WITHDRAWN

ILLINOIS CENTRAL COLLEGE
PS3529.G39
C.2        STACKS
A dancer in yellow /

A12900 389224

PS 3529 .G39

Ogilvie, Elisab

A dancer in yellow /

WITHDRAWN

Illinois Central College
Learning Resources Center

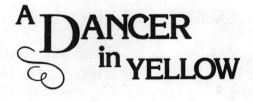

# A Dancer in Yellow

## BOOKS BY ELISABETH OGILVIE

A Dancer in Yellow
An Answer in the Tide
The Dreaming Swimmer
Where the Lost Aprils Are
Image of a Lover
Strawberries in the Sea
Weep and Know Why
A Theme for Reason
The Face of Innocence
Bellwood
Waters on a Starry Night

The Seasons Hereafter
There May Be Heaven
Call Home the Heart
The Witch Door
High Tide at Noon
Storm Tide
The Ebbing Tide
Rowan Head
My World Is an Island
The Dawning of the Day
No Evil Angel

## BOOKS FOR YOUNG PEOPLE

The Pigeon Pair
Masquerade at Sea House
Ceiling of Amber
Turn Around Twice
Becky's Island
The Young Islanders
How Wide the Heart
Blueberry Summer
Whistle for a Wind
The Fabulous Year
Come Aboard and Bring
    Your Dory!

# A DANCER in YELLOW

## By Elisabeth Ogilvie

McGraw-Hill Book Company

NEW YORK  ST. LOUIS  SAN FRANCISCO
TORONTO  DÜSSELDORF  MEXICO

I. C. C.  LIBRARY          68399

Copyright © 1979 by Elisabeth Ogilvie. All rights reserved.
Printed in the United States of America. No part of this
publication may be reproduced, stored in a retrieval system,
or transmitted in any form or by any means, electronic,
mechanical, photocopying, recording, or otherwise, without
the written permission of the publisher.

123456789 BPBP 7832109


LIBRARY OF CONGRESS CATALOGING IN PUBLICATION DATA

Ogilvie, Elisabeth, date
A dancer in yellow.
I.  Title.
PZ3.0348Dan      [PS3529.G39]      813'.5'2      78-23852
ISBN 0-07-047600-4

Book design by Roberta Rezk

"O! There is sweet music on yonder green hill, O!
And you shall be a dancer, a dancer in yellow,
All in yellow, all in yellow,"
Said the crow to the frog, and then, O!
"All in yellow, all in yellow,"
Said the frog to the crow again, O!

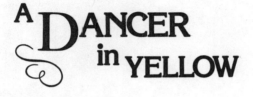

# Chapter
# 1

It was near midnight, and there were fog patches along the road, suddenly and blindingly flooding the hollows. Each time it was as if the car went overboard and submerged, and each time Astrid expected that all at once other headlights would confront them on the rise, an enormous dazzling glow in the mist, and there would be instant and messy dissolution.

Yet it wasn't really different from many other spring nights when they'd driven home late. If anything, it was better, since they now had the yellow line to steer by. And the chance of meeting someone driving smack in the middle of the road when you came around a corner or over a rise was a fact of life along any country road; Gray knew it and kept well to the side. He'd been a careful driver ever since he got his first car.

So why this constant upsurge and down-plunge in her stomach, this claustrophobia in the fog, this apprehension like a bad attack of second sight?

I'm just bushed, she told herself. Their days began at daylight, and besides tending house and the children, she was working hard at getting the garden ready. She'd also added a few layers to the woodpile and thus diminished the load of hardwood Gray had brought out of the woods before the frost left. She'd always been handier with an ax than with the piano, a talent that caused her parents much grief.

She tackled everything with special gusto now that it was May; no wonder she was tired tonight on top of all the work. She conjured up a pleasant image of their bed under its prismatic quilt, an oasis of peace and privacy until dawn returned too fast.

They were driving along a clear space now, and the sound of the peepers in an alder swamp burst loudly upon her ears over the soft rush of the tires. The chill damp pungencies of the spring night and the nearby but unseen ocean blew into the car. . . . Bed, with Gray; the touching all night and the sleepy embrace of. waking. She was bone-tired. A *good* tired.

Not quite a good tired, though. On other nights, lulled to drowsiness, she'd move over against Gray as he drove; they might talk, or be silent as they'd been for most of the ride tonight, but either way the communication would be there. Tonight she had the feeling that Gray's silence was anything but relaxed and that he wouldn't welcome being touched even by her.

There'd been a moment during the evening when she'd looked across the room and seen him withdrawn from the conversation, withdrawn from the *place* as much as a man could be without physically moving, and the sight of his face had been like a punch in her belly. *He looks sick!* She had almost cried it aloud. Sick and worried about it; it frightened her; it was like the first realization that one of the children wasn't well and the terror that roiled her insides even while she was taking the necessary steps. She would show nothing outwardly, but Gray always knew and managed by a glance or a touch to drive her panic away. He was one of seven and knew that a temperature didn't necessarily herald a rare and fatal disease.

But there'd been no one to reassure her about Gray in that instant, and in the next he was laughing at something, and she decided that hollowed, grayish, anxious look had been a trick of the light. For the rest of the evening she'd tried to keep from watching for it and had succeeded. By the time they'd left their friends' house, she was convinced that her tendency to alarmism needed to be ruthlessly squelched, or she'd be old before her time.

And then, once they were driving home, the thing had come to squat blackly in the car with them, like the apparition in *Green Tea*.

There *was* something wrong. Lately he hadn't been eating or sleeping the way he should. She'd been trying to ride it out, waiting for him to tell her in his own good time what was bothering him. But from that one giveaway look tonight she knew they couldn't wait any longer. There'd be no pussyfooting but one swift attack taking him by surprise.

"*Gray*," she said, and the attack was spoiled because her voice came out froggy with nerves and self-consciousness. She cleared her throat and said sternly, "Gray, what's wrong?"

"Wrong?" It was too fast, and the amusement was false. "What do you mean, wrong?"

"You don't feel well. Is it in your mind or your insides or both?" He wasn't too young to have cancer; maybe he was so afraid that he couldn't talk about it. Her own mouth was dry. She put her hand on his arm. "Whatever it is, Gray, it belongs to me, too, and the children. They can't help, but I can."

His arm was rigid. He didn't speak and they swung around a curve into another pocket of swirling mist, their beam bouncing confusingly back at them. Then they were out of it and not far from their own turn-off.

"There is something," Gray said at last. "On my mind, not on my gut."

She let her breath go, audibly. "*That's* a relief. What's the trouble? Is it the firm? Look, Gray, any time you want to make a change I'm with you, you know that."

"If Fletch wasn't so damned good it would be a lot easier. And Cam's all right too, even if I do get fed up with the so-called humor. I guess I do have gut trouble. Lack of guts. I just can't stand up and say, I'm walking out because I can't take being the kid brother any longer."

"They'd understand. Just ask them how they'd like being the youngest all their lives."

"They haven't got that much imagination."

"Never mind that, then," Astrid said. "If you're going on your own, now's the time. Their feelings might be hurt for a little while, Fletch's anyway, but when they see how well you do on your own, they'll be glad for you."

"How well will I do on my own?" he asked harshly.

So that was it: self-doubt.

"You're a skilled carpenter. You can get work anywhere, either on your own or with another firm. And I know how to squeeze the nickels like crazy," she said proudly.

He said with affection, "Ayuh, you do fine for a spoiled little rich kid."

"I was little once, but not spoiled and not rich," she objected happily and slid her hand inside his elbow. The black presence had left the car. Gray turned into their road. It sloped gently down through the spruces toward the black and starlit shimmer of the cove. The illuminated windows of their house cast an unreal radiance, as if the house itself were filled with a golden other-wordly light.

"She's all lit up as if she just discovered electricity," Gray complained sourly.

"Maybe she's nervous," said Astrid. "She was telling me once she was afraid the Cades might bother her some-times. Is Kevin's car there?" She tried to make it out in the shadows of the barn.

"I don't know." Gray was still annoyed. "I never thought it was a good idea for a sitter to have boys in. I don't want to take a chance on the children seeing any-thing they shouldn't."

"Kevin's a good kid and a responsible one," Astrid said. "And if he's here it means he can drive her home. I hate to have you go on that Swedetown road in the middle of the night. I'm always afraid somebody'll be drag-racing out there, or you'll meet some drunk spang in the middle of the sawmill bridge, or a truckful of Cades rushing away from their latest vandalism."

"Oh good God! Calamity Jane!" They both laughed, but she was half serious.

"I can't help it. These awful things do happen right out of nowhere, you know that."

"Listen, love. I've been driving these roads for fifteen

years man and boy. There've always been drunks and drag-racing and truckloads of hellions, but the nearest I've come to any of 'em was the time I happened to see some jacking going on in Hank Barlow's pasture and called the sheriff's patrol on my CB."

"And got them arrested so they've been laying for you ever since."

"I think that in five years that particular bunch has forgotten about getting even with me."

"Well, *I* haven't forgotten the telephone calls. Not completely. I was carrying Peter then, and I thought he was going to be marked by it."

"Take my advice, honeybunch, and forget them for good. There are a lot worse things in life than a few phone calls from some of Amity's prize morons. They never did what they threatened, did they?"

"No, dear." She yawned in comfortable anticipation of the warm bright house. As they reached it the headlights showed an empty drive, and he stopped the car at the back door instead of driving into the attached barn.

"No Kevin," she said. "Darn! Well, maybe it won't be so foggy inland a way."

He pulled her head toward him and gave her a rough, fervent kiss. "Will you get out? Or do you want to drive the sitter home so you won't fuss about what *I'm* doing?"

"If we had a dog-nurse like the one in *Peter Pan* we could both go." She got out. "Are you coming in?"

"No, send her out. It's been a long day and I'd like to get it over with."

She stopped by his window. "Don't fall asleep at the wheel."

"No chance. That one's always bright as a flash bulb at midnight."

"I mean on the way back."

He smiled and put his finger on her nose. "I'll keep thinking of you." His narrow dark face was intent and somber in repose, so that when he smiled the complete change could still take her by surprise, and she would feel again the palpitations and dazzle of first love. Which had turned out to be the only love, she thought blissfully, going into the house.

Dorri, the sitter, was rinsing a mug and a plate at the kitchen sink. She'd been named Doris, which she hated, and had gone for the short-"i" diminutive when she was about twelve. She smiled around at Astrid through curtains of shimmering brown hair straight and smooth as polished birch, her eyes tawny and luminous in a sharply chiseled little face. She was slender, fine-boned, practically hipless in her skin-tight jeans.

"Every time I see you I wish I was tall!" she exclaimed. "And the way you wear clothes—I love that outfit!"

"Well, thanks, Dorri. It's just a little thing I ran up out of some old grain bags."

Dorri giggled. "Did you have a nice evening?"

"Lovely. How was yours?"

"Okay. Kevin never showed, so I got no help on my geometry, but the boys were angels. We sang, and that got them good and sleepy. But Peter got teed off with me because there was one I didn't know. Something about a frog and a crow?"

Astrid laughed. " 'The Frog and the Crow.' Yes, it's his favorite right now. He loves frogs, and someday he'll find out the crow ate the frog at the end, and that'll be a tragedy." She helped Dorri load up with her books and heavily bulging shoulder bag. "I guess Gray'll pay you when he drops you off. If he doesn't, remind him."

"Oh, he's never cheated me yet. Wow, Saturday morning again! Do I love to *sleep!*"

"Enjoy it while you can," said Astrid. "When you're married and have kids those days are gone forever."

"Like the days of wine and roses in the song." They stood in the open doorway, letting in the night scents and the sound of the idling car. "Night, Astrid," Dorri said. "Have a nice weekend."

"You too. And thanks, Dorri."

The girl smiled and ran down the few steps to the car. A door slammed, and the car went out with a soft shush of tires on gravel. Astrid shut the house door before the tail lights had disappeared beyond the spruces and looked at her kitchen with the pleasure of homecoming. They had modernized it without taking away its spacious old-fashioned farmhouse character. No cold white fluorescent lights for them, and there was room for a rocking chair and a black iron range, which they used whenever the power failed so that the heater went off. It was for this stove and the living-room fireplace that she'd been working up wood that afternoon.

She went up the back stairs from the kitchen into the bedroom Gray had made for the boys in the open chamber. Christian was three and Peter was just past four. They looked as angelic as Dorri had described them, in the sound sleep of healthy children. Chris, named for Astrid's father, had the neat, dark, all-together Price look, while Peter

Graham Price had the appearance of a Scandinavian athlete-to-be.

"Huckleberries and cream, those two," a very old Price aunt had said. "Same as you and their father."

She went through the spare room and across the hall into her and Gray's big room. It looked on the water, and with nothing out there she hadn't bothered to draw the shades. She turned on a lamp and undressed, tidily hanging up her clothes and walking barefoot over the braided rugs and the smoothly finished planks with a tactile pleasure in the change of surfaces beneath her soles and in the air on her naked body. She was a tall, broad-shouldered young woman with a Nordic face and fair hair worn short and dark-blue eyes. She had a quiet, shy-seeming manner; it had been genuine shyness once, before Graham.

History's definitive initials were B.C. Astrid's were B.G. Before Graham.

She put on her pajamas and robe and went down by the front stairs this time for the satisfaction of the white-balustered flight and a look into the long living room. They'd made it into something entirely different from what it was in her parents' day, when it had been an extension of their Boston studio, dominated by the grand piano that to small Astrid had the malevolent personality of a large and sulking black bear. They used to have it trucked down and back each summer. Now she had a small spinet.

And so back into the kitchen again. Twenty of one. Gray had been gone nearly half an hour. He should be on his way home by now. She would make cocoa in a saucepan; he liked that better than the instant kind. She began singing softly the song that had been going through her head ever since Dorri had mentioned it.

" 'O! There is sweet music on yonder green hill, O!
And you shall be a dancer, a dancer in yellow,
All in yellow, all in yellow,'
Said the crow to the frog, and then, O!
'All in yellow, all in yellow,'
Said the frog to the crow again, O!"

She smiled sadly. Poor Peter, when he realized the frog never reached the other side and the sweet music on yonder green hill. She remembered how she'd howled when she found out what really happened to Clementine.

# Chapter 2

At half past one Gray wasn't back yet. He could be standing in the Sears kitchen yarning with Rupert and Carrie. More likely Carrie; Rupe would be in bed, if he was going out to haul at dawn. Carrie liked to talk and she was hard to escape. Gray used to come home swearing that the Sears women didn't know night from day.

She tried to settle down to reading in the rocking chair, but an evil vision flashed across her mind of a car breaking in slow motion through the railing on the sawmill bridge and toppling into the flooded stream. It was far away from houses, among woodlots and overgrown fields. In the middle of the night, who was to know about it except the driver of the car that forced the other one off? And who in terror and guilt wouldn't be likely to do or say anything but would just race off?

Or suppose it was a thick patch of fog hanging over the stream, making the little slope to the bridge hard to find? There was no yellow line on the Swedetown road.

"Oh, you fool!" she said aloud. "He's trying to get away from Carrie." But her heartbeat was hard and heavy. This was how death came out of nowhere. She was across the room to the telephone without thinking whom to call. Graham's voice teased. *Calamity Jane. Worrywart.* "All right for you!" she said to him. "You'll hate this, but I can't help it."

He had left here about quarter past twelve, and it was now almost two. She dialed the Searses' number and Carrie answered at once. "Hello! What is it?" It was like a hostile leap through the phone. She's scared too, Astrid thought.

"It's Astrid, Carrie," she said, sounding calm. "If Gray's there, don't tell him I'm checking, but I worry about the bridge and things in the middle of the night."

"He's not here!" Her voice was heavier than Dorri's, but it had the same ingenuous, almost sexless, brightness. "I was just about to call *you*. I thought she was parked somewhere with Kevin."

"No, Gray took her home, and they left here about an hour and a half ago." Astrid's jaw felt funny, and it took an effort to measure the words out evenly. "I'd better call someone."

"No, look, I'll get Rupe up and we'll go look. Gray's likely got a flat tire out in the woods somewhere. He may be walking her home for all we know." She was resolutely cheerful. "I'll call you. Oh! Here they are!" she sang out jubilantly. "The car's just coming into the yard. It's his, all right. I've got the outside light on and I can see."

"Good." Astrid shut her eyes and sagged against the wall. "Remember, don't tell him I called."

"No, and I won't let him hang around here talking either. 'Night!" She hung up. Astrid smiled weakly. Gray would love that crack; too bad she couldn't share it with him.

In a half hour he had put the car away and was coming in through the shed from the barn, squinting at the light in the kitchen, black brows drawn in a scowl. "I suppose you had me drowned, cracked up, or slugged by the Cades," he said sardonically.

"Part of the time, dear. But I should have known you're wearing your Superman underwear. Want some hot cocoa?"

"No, thanks." He dropped his coat over a chair. "Whatever Dinah had in that sauce tonight, it's still with me."

"Nothing ever used to bother you. You could always eat the damnedest things. If the firm's doing this to you, it's time for you to quit."

"Well, I don't want to talk about it tonight."

"What did happen out there? Flat tire?"

"You know what I said about the Sears women not knowing night from day. That kid wanted to detour all around Robin Hood's barn to leave a book." He went into the bathroom and came out crunching a Maalox tablet. "I said, 'For Pete's sake, the people'll be in *bed!*' and she said, 'Oh, Roxie won't be.' "

"Roxie Manning?"

"That's right. Well, Roxie had to have the book to get her homework done for Monday, and she had some complicated yarn about why Roxie couldn't get it tomorrow, so like a damn fool I swung off at the fork to go to Mannings'. And Roxie was up." He nodded savagely at Astrid. "Yeah, she was up. Just got home from a date, I guess. And they're yakking their heads off as if it's high noon while I'm slowly sinking into a coma."

"Darling, I'm sorry," she said. "Now can you see why I don't mind her having Kevin here?"

"Oh, sure," he said wearily. "I just don't like the thought of them making out on the living-room couch and Peter coming downstairs for something."

"But I don't automatically suspect the worst of teen-agers, especially those two. Dorri's told me herself how disgusted she is with a lot of the stuff that's going on." She put her hands on his shoulders. "You're passing out on your feet. Go on to bed, and don't worry about anything. And this weekend we'll talk about the future."

He had kept his heavy eyes on her face as she spoke, with a sort of resigned passivity, almost a sadness, that would have bothered her more if he hadn't already told her what was on his mind. It stabbed her now, but at least they could do something about it. She kissed him. "I'll be up in a few minutes. I've got all waked up."

He left her without a word. She reheated the cocoa and poured out a cupful and sipped it slowly, staring at nothing. He would have to break away from the family firm when it had brought him to this state of nerves. It was tragic, because he loved his older brothers. But she'd read that sometimes a last child had special problems. Gray might have been secretly resenting the older ones all these years and feeling guilty for resenting them, until it all broke out like a virus surfacing.

They'll understand, she thought. Or they'll try to. They're not a mean family. We can live on clams and mussels and pollock and the garden, raise a pig—no, that was out; the boys wouldn't stand for it being killed and she didn't know if she could go through that either. Smiling, she rinsed out her cup and went to brush her teeth. We could have hens for the eggs, though; they'd love that.

Gray seemed to be asleep when she slid in beside him, so she tried not to disturb him. She put herself to sleep by going fishing in the cove on a summer day, all four of them in the big safe old dory. The only trouble was that the boys didn't want the fish to die.

She woke up at her usual time with the sunrise coming in and the gulls shouting. Gray was already up. She rose groggily, already yearning for the boys' naptime. There was something relentless about a spring sunrise, with all nature in full cry when you weren't ready for it.

The boys didn't get the sunrise in their room, and still slept. With luck, she'd have her coffee before they woke. She felt her way down the front stairs, sniffing for coffee, but apparently Gray hadn't made any. She looked from habit into the living room and saw him sleeping on the couch with her grandfather's tartan steamer rug over him. His face was turned to the back of the sofa; she saw only part of his black head and a hunched shoulder.

Her angry tenderness woke her completely. Darling, I won't let you go on like this! she thought.

She washed sleep out of her eyes and made the coffee as quietly as possible. The table was at the big new window that overlooked the cove, and she sat there with her coffee. No month was as beautiful as May here, she believed, and now it was beginning, and they should all be as happy as kings rarely were.... Oh my, Astrid, you're really a simple girl with a one-track mind. Gray has to be helped, and then we can begin to enjoy May.

He appeared in a few minutes, muttered Hello, and went into the bathroom. When he came out, shaved and hair combed, she had coffee poured for him.

"I'll take it upstairs while I dress," he said. "Don't fix anything else." His color was not good, his manner distracted.

"Couldn't you sleep?" she asked. "Was it mental or physical indigestion?"

"Some of both." He gave her a slight, nervous grin. "It'll pass."

"I'm pretty slow myself today. You'd think we both got smashed last night and had hangovers this morning," she joked.

He murmured something and left with his coffee cup. She was disappointed not to have a little while alone with him, but he was obviously in no shape for a discussion.

The firm was working on Saturdays to get the house finished by June, and they liked to be on the job by seven. This morning the boys weren't awake by the time Gray left; their songfest the night before must have gone on well past their bedtime. Usually they saw their father out to the truck and had a quick kiss and a hug. Today everything was knocked out of focus somehow; with Gray's problems on her mind and giving her a queasy stomach in sympathy with his, Astrid completely forgot his lunch until he was gone. She had received her kiss, they had embraced by the door, his arms tight, his face in her neck, and then he seemed to be gone so fast it was almost as if he'd been swept away from her by a feat of black magic.

She knew it was going to be like an amputation to cut himself off from the brothers; she knew that at the same time he had to be his own man. We'll take care of it this weekend, she thought resolutely. Sunday will be The Day when we take charge of our own lives. Of course he'd finish out this job, but he shouldn't delay talking to them about the break; the uncertainty and the anticipation were killing him.

Peter woke up cranky, ready to cry when he knew Gray had gone. Chris took his mood from his older brother. She cheered them up by saying they'd take Gray's lunch to him on the job. Then they couldn't wait but followed her around trying to hurry her up. She refused to let them manage her, though with Peter it was uphill all the way.

In midmorning she took out a carton of frozen home-made clam chowder, heated it just under the boiling point, and put it in a wide-mouth thermos container; clam chowder was one of Gray's favorite meals. He wouldn't want dessert. He wasn't much for sweets and she was glad of that; she was proud of his lean, neat build. She made coffee and included a batch of applesauce cookies for the other men.

The new house was being built on a point jutting southwesterly into the sea. It looked to be mostly decks, glass, and gables at odd angles, but it was beginning to belong with the granite ledges, the bay and juniper and spruces.

Gray was up on the highest ridgepole, sharply outlined against the dapple of warm cloud and blue sky. He waved his hammer at the shouting children, and even from this distance Astrid could see the smile; it was as if someone had just cut a noose that had been crushing in her ribs, and suddenly she felt light enough to leave the ground. The boys were running around the site like sandpipers on the beach and had discovered Cam working on the shoreward side, so they weren't at the ladder when Gray came down. Fletch was inside somewhere.

"Are you all right?" she said in a low voice.

"Now I am." He put his arm around her.

"Have you talked to them, then?" she asked eagerly. He shook his head, still smiling. "No, but it'll be all right. It came to me a little while ago, while I was up there with all that sea spread out before me. A feeling that everything would go fine. I was really on top of things, no pun intended."

She kissed him quickly and was almost caught by Fletcher Price, who came out looking benignly at her over his glasses. "Who's distracting my crew?"

"I came all the way down here to bring you something you like for your coffee break, Fletch."

"Ah! That's different, then. It's time for a coffee break right now." He was dark like Graham, but bigger, and he never hurried, whereas Gray was always quick. He was four years older than Gray, but with his placid manner verging on stolidity he had always seemed much older, grown up even back when Astrid had first met the Price brothers. She'd been twelve years old, and their father had done some remodeling on the house at the cove for her father.

Fletch went to his truck to get his thermos bottle, and Cam came around the house with Chris and Peter. He was a year younger than Fletch, another dark-eyed, black-haired Price, but one that was always whistling and full of jokes to suit whatever audience he had at the moment. Now he had the boys chuckling at some piece of humor they found perfectly understandable. He kissed Astrid and said, "We've got to stop meeting like this. Your husband's going to catch on."

"I came to ask you to elope with me," said Astrid. "My bag's all packed and in the car."

"But I couldn't go without my toothbrush and my special cologne."

"Niggle, niggle, niggle, that's him," said Gray, distributing cookies to the boys.

"We never have to worry about Cam taking off without warning," said Fletch. "He couldn't run away without all his beauty aids."

"Unless he makes it with the Avon Lady," Gray suggested.

It was a pleasant half hour there on the deck, and she drove home in a happy frame of mind. The boys were ready to settle down and play with their trucks in the sand pile beside the barn. After lunch Sam Bearse came to plow up the new place in the field where she wanted to plant potatoes, and that postponed naps but kept the children in fascinated silence while they watched from the front steps.

Before Sam was through, Kevin Whitehouse drove in. He was eighteen, a very tall boy who sometimes seemed shambly and uncoordinated, but this was probably due to self-consciousness, because he was an excellent ballplayer and had been approached by several colleges because of it. He was on his way to play now in a school game.

"All alone?" Astrid asked him.

"Oh, she'll be at the game. She's going with some other girls." He blushed; the mere mention of Dorri apparently did this to him these days. "I just stopped by for—Gray home?" He was looking down past the garden and the man on the tractor toward the old fishhouse and wharf at the cove. He squinted against the glare, and his Adam's apple moved up and down.

He had a gentle, bony face, transparently showing whatever he felt. No one could call him handsome now, but someday, Astrid believed, he would be a distinguished-looking man. His features were strong, he was both intelligent and good as far as she knew, and a little adult poise and self-assurance could pull everything together with great results.

"Gray's working. Something on your mind, Kevin?" she asked him.

He squinted even harder and scrubbed at his creased forehead with his knuckles. "Not really," he said. "I'm trying to round up some extra summer jobs. I'll be working at the store, but I'll need every cent I can get. You've got a lot of lawn here, and ..." He was embarrassed to be asking.

"Well, I don't mind mowing," she said, "and neither does Gray, but there comes a time when it gets to be a nuisance, with all the other summer projects around here. Sure, I'd like to have you mow, Kevin."

He smiled. "Thanks, Astrid. When do you want me to start?"

"Oh, wait till after graduation. You must have a lot of stuff going on right now."

"We do," he admitted. "Okay, then, it's a date. Thanks an awful lot, Astrid." He started back toward his car, then turned and gave her an awkward little salute. She watched him go, trying to imagine Chris and Peter at that age. She was glad Dorri appreciated him. The girl was as charming and ornamental as a young cat, and she probably could have had her choice among some of the more glamorous males at Williston High, but she had the intelligence—or intuition—to realize what was genuine.

After that bit of contented philosophizing Astrid turned her thoughts happily toward Gray's return that night, a whole Sunday all their own, and the beginning of May, her favorite month of the year.

Gray still looked cheerful when he came home. He took a shower and changed and played with the boys while she got supper on. Afterward he gave them baths and put them to bed; having missed their naps, they didn't last through more than two pages of Peter Rabbit's adventures.

When they were deeply asleep, Gray and Astrid walked down to the cove and sat on the overturned dory to watch the sunset colors grow and change over the water. They talked about the garden, about the usual things they looked forward to doing in summer—getting the dory ready to go overboard, trolling for mackerel, picnics on the islands outside.

"And we ought to get the skiff down from the loft in the fishhouse," Astrid said. "Peter wants to learn to row this summer. Maybe we could get her down tomorrow, and then I could scrape her in my spare time."

"Anyone can tell you're a foreigner," he teased her. "Don't you know you should never start anything on a Sunday?"

"Seems to me we started Peter on a Sunday," she said demurely, "and there's nothing wrong with that job."

He laughed. "He's a great kid. I just wish your father could have lived to see him. He's the spit'n' image of big Chris."

"And little Chris is a Welshman. I wish *your* father could see *him.*"

They walked back to the house in the afterglow, arms around each other's waists. He seemed more at peace with himself and with her than he had been for a long time.

Robins scolded from the woods, and song sparrows performed their evening chorale. The peepers were starting their night song in the alder swamps. Any day now the first white-throats would be heard.

"I ought to hang you a May basket, Gray," Astrid said dreamily as they came around to the back door. In the kitchen the wall telephone began to ring and Gray automatically ran up the steps. "Just what did you intend to hang it *on?*" he called back to her, laughing, and went inside. They'd read *Lady Chatterley's Lover* and found certain portions of it hilarious.

As she came through the door, trying to think of a good answer, he was saying, "Mullarkey's Bar! Whoever you want, he's just been arrested. There's a police raid going on right now." She began to take the clean dishes out of the drainer, imagining one of his firemen or poker-playing friends on the other end. She tried to guess what Zeke or Monty would think of to go along with the joke—Gray would presently come away from the telephone and tell her—and then she realized how very quiet he was. He stood there listening and staring at the wall before him. He was not smiling; he was so still, so apart from her, so absolutely concentrated on what he was hearing, that she thought at once, *He's getting bad news.*

It was either in his family, or it was her mother, who seemed indestructible; but so had many of the airplanes that later exploded or crashed, and her mother traveled so much by air that one saw her darting like a bright sleek fish among the catastrophes.

Finally Gray said tiredly, "All right. I'll be there." Slowly he replaced the telephone. She came out of her paralysis and ran to him. "Gray, what's wrong? Who's hurt? Who was that?"

"Nobody's hurt." The iron heaviness was still in him. "Look, I can't talk now. I'll tell you later."

He left her so fast that her hand was knocked off his arm. She followed him to the door, speechless, and watched him back the truck around and start up the lane. All she could think of now was that something had happened to the house they were building. Maybe it was on fire! She ran back to the telephone and called Fletch's number. One of the children answered.

"It's Aunt Astrid, Hughie. Are your parents home?"

"Hi, Aunt Astrid. They're both here. Which one do you want?"

"Either. Oh, your mother, I guess."

Nora came on, heartily. "Hello! Isn't this nice? You two driving over? I was just saying to Fletch, people don't drop in these days the way they used to. They all got TV programs they can't miss." She laughed. Obviously there wasn't any trouble.

"Oh, we had a night out last night, and we can't make it two nights in a row," Astrid said. "I just thought I'd say hello."

"I'm glad you did. When are you bringing the boys over? How about lunch Monday?"

"I'd love it," said Astrid. They talked for a few minutes. Nora was so bouncily matter-of-fact that she gave off an aura of strength and sanity, and Astrid began to believe that she'd imagined Gray's manner. Maybe one of his friends was in a jam.

"No sense saying see you in church," Nora said breezily

at the end. She and Fletch attended a strict fundamentalist group that had splintered off from the local Congregationalist church and formed a church of its own with some Amity dissidents. She and Fletch were neither smug nor critical, however.

"Well, I do get the boys to Sunday school here even if I can't drag Gray to a service," Astrid said.

"Oh, he'll come back to it when he needs it," Nora said comfortably. "What's bred in the bone comes out in the flesh. The Prices have always been religious; the first one who came over from Wales was a preacher, remember." She lowered her voice. "Sometimes I think Fletch is a reincarnation of the old boy." They both laughed and said good night. Astrid now felt immensely better. Then she thought that it was Cameron who called; he'd had a drink too many and either had gone off the road somewhere or had hit another car.

Oh, brother, wait till Fletch hears about it, Astrid thought. A Price in the court news for driving under the influence. Well, it was a wonder it hadn't happened earlier. Cam had the most outward charm of the three and the most sociable disposition. Poor Cam, poor Harriet, who sometimes felt his sociability was too much of a good thing.

Well, if nobody's hurt we'll probably all live through it, Astrid thought. Cam will be repentant for a while, and Harriet will put her chin up and defy anyone to say *one word* about him, or even raise an eyebrow, and whatever Fletch says to Cam in private we'll never know.

She arranged herself to watch a play on TV, but she couldn't really concentrate; it was like last night when Gray was late. But that was all for nothing, she told herself. Still, when he hadn't come back or called by half past nine, she walked the floor wondering whether or not to call Harriet. But if Cam *was* in trouble, she shouldn't bother Harriet. Damn you, Gray, she thought angrily, why don't *you* call?

She went upstairs finally and lay on the bed. The extension telephone was mute under the lamp, and she fell asleep finally simply because she was too tired to stay awake.

Gulls woke her at first light, banking past the windows and calling to one another. She was alone in the bed. She was instantly frightened and hurried downstairs. Gray was lying on the sofa again, this time uncovered, still dressed, his hands behind his head. He was staring at the ceiling. He moved his eyes toward her; otherwise his face was like stone. She sank to her knees beside him and laid her hand on his chest.

"Gray, what's wrong? What's happened? Was it Cam?"

"*Cam?*" He looked bewildered.

"That's all I could think of last night. He'd been arrested or something."

"No." He moved his head restlessly.

"Then what was the call? Who's in trouble? Zeke or Monty?"

"Nothing like that."

He turned his head away from her, staring at the flowered back of the sofa. She began to feel very cold and the chill had nothing to do with the early morning.

"Gray, will you tell me what's wrong?" Her voice was soft because she hadn't the strength to speak any other way.

"Let me sit up." She drew her hand away and moved over on the rug. He rose up, swung his legs down, and sat with his elbows on his knees and his head in his hands. "I don't know how to tell you this," he said.

"Tell me what?" She pressed her fist against the sickening palpitations in her chest.

"I'm going away," he said to the rug.

"Where do you want us to go?"

"I said 'I.' "

The monstrous cold iced down her panic. "You'd better start at the beginning," she said. "Because one of us is crazy, and I'm afraid it's me."

"No." He lowered his hands and looked wearily into her face. "I've been lying here all night thinking how to tell you, and there's no easy way. I'm going away with Dorri."

# Chapter 3

She put her hands on his knees and said, "What did you say?"

"I don't want to say it again."

"You have to. Or I won't believe you ever said it."

"Oh, I said it all right." He put his hands over hers. "I wish—Oh Christ, Astrid." He took her by the wrists and pushed her forcefully away from him and got up.

She said with infinite care, "You and *Dorri?* You're having . . . *You?*" There was the beating in her chest and a worse one in her head. She was afraid of blacking out and then wished she would.

"Will you get the hell up off your knees?" he cried savagely at her. She lifted herself onto the sofa, knowing her legs wouldn't hold her. He stood against the fireplace. His voice was trembling. "Look, I have to go now. We'll talk later, okay?"

"Go where?"

"She's waiting for me. I don't want her calling here again."

"She called last night?" The words hardly came out, as if her laboring lungs couldn't deliver the breath for them.

"Yes. She'd had a bad row with her folks and they put her out, so I had to go. She's in a motel now. She's in terrible shape. I can't leave her there like that."

"The other night..." Now she was trembling as the impressions rushed rapidly at her. Dorri smiling, the luminous eyes and the ingenuous admiration; the fine-boned, fresh-colored, virginal gaiety. "The other night, all the time we were talking... All the time since *when?*"

"I don't know how far back! It doesn't matter. It's a fact. It's happened. I never intended it to go this far—believe me, Astrid, I was going to call it off, and I did, the other night. We talked and talked. I thought she'd accepted it."

"Is she pregnant?"

"Good God, no!" He recoiled as if she'd offended him. "I'm not that irresponsible!"

"You could have fooled me." She sat staring into the cold fireplace, shivering in crescendos, and suddenly he swooped over her, trying clumsily to bundle the steamer rug around her.

"Listen, I want to be gone before the kids wake up. But I'll be back when we've both calmed down. Do you hear me, Astrid?" He sounded as if he'd been running. Objectively she knew he was suffering, but she could feel nothing except her own violent physical reactions. Was it possible for anyone to die from such a shock? *The kids*, he'd said. She couldn't die and leave them. She forced her breathing to deepen, but she still couldn't look up at him.

"I don't want to leave you like this," he said despairingly. "You look awful. I'll call somebody to be with you."

"No! I don't want anybody to know about it. Then when it's over it'll be over. You said it was over, didn't you? Whatever it was?" She could hear her voice tinny in her head.

"The Searses know; she told them last night. And some of her friends know. I told her to keep it quiet, but she's so much of a kid . . ." As if he were conscious that his own words condemned him, he shut up abruptly and walked out. She huddled into the steamer rug, wanting to shriek out her plea for them both to wake up and go back to the instant before he had said the words, and then not say them. But they were all around the room, in letters both visible and audible. *I'm going away with Dorri.*

He was back in the doorway, a coat over his arm and carrying a zipper satchel. "I'll take the pick-up," he said, "and leave you the car. Astrid, get something hot in your stomach." She couldn't look directly at him. He was a blurred presence from the corner of her eye.

"Why do you have to go?" she cried. "For *her?* What about *me?*" But he didn't answer. The whole scene had taken less than a half hour. The part that had killed her had come in the first five words. It was the unexpected accident she had always feared, except that there was no instant eclipse. She remained where she was, still half believing the truck would come plunging back down the road and he'd hurry to her, crying out his foolishness and misery. But he didn't come, and there was no chance of her waking up to sunny reality. The sunrise was already happening, and she was already awake.

The consciousness of the children roused her, and she moved fast. A cold shower, though she usually loathed them, brought her abrasively to life. Then hot coffee. While she was dressing she heard the children's voices across the hall. Peter always woke up on Sundays with Sunday school on his mind. He was a sociable child and loved being with other children. So she couldn't escape that. In fact, with two small children there was no escape from anything.

Peter dressed himself and helped Chris and would have determinedly scrubbed his brother's face and fought the snarls out of his hair if Astrid hadn't taken over. The routine, the contact with them, was tranquilizing, at least on the surface, as long as she just kept thinking of that and not allowing anything else to surface. But it was there all right, and even without looking at it she knew it was becoming even more dreadful and incredible all the time. The squatting black presence in the car really existed.

"Where's Daddy?" Peter asked all at once. "Down to the shore?"

Chris ran to look out. "Digging clams?" he asked eagerly. "I can help."

"The tide's too high," Peter told him.

"Daddy has to work today," she said. "They're trying to get the new house ready for the people." They accepted that. Peter wasn't old enough yet to realize that Fletch would never work on a Sunday.

She waited in the churchyard to see the boys going in, Peter tightly holding Chris's hand. They would be kept in afterward until parents called for them. She drove on down the road to the public landing and bought a Sunday paper, which she usually loathed, and sat there with the paper propped against the wheel so she'd look like an ordinary person waiting for someone. She found after a while that she was thinking more clearly; she was even wondering where Gray was and if he were tormented by remorse, guilt, apprehension at what he had started. Or if in that mysterious motel somewhere he had said, "To hell with them all!"

But she could not make herself imagine him making love to Dorri. She could function only by concentrating on Gray and nobody else, or she would really explode.

She drove back when it was time. She had to get out of the car to let the woman in charge know she was there. Church was beginning; as she walked around to the wing where the Sunday-school classes met, the first hymn burst enthusiastically from open windows. "Fair are the meadows; fairer still the woodlands, Clothed in the blooming garb of spring. . . ."

She had always loved it. But not any more, not after today.

Lunch was a picnic on the shore, which meant that the boys entertained themselves sailing their boats in the tide pools and she had only to admire or comment in the right places. By now she felt as if she'd been without sleep for a week which had begun at five this morning. She ached to sink softly into unconsciousness and wake up to find it was all over—bruised, lacerated, still aching in places, but *whole*. Which meant being with Gray.

They used up a couple of hours before Chris came to lean heavily against her, and Peter started to slow down. "Come on," she said briskly. "Let's all take a nap and be nice and fresh for supper."

"When Daddy comes!" said Peter. "Maybe we can turn over the dory and go for a row."

"We've got to scrape her and paint her first," she said. "So we won't be going for a row tonight."

"Then let's start fixing her up tomorrow. And the skiff!" He remembered suddenly. "You said I could have the *skiff*."

"We'll see. Let's get our naps now. Go to the bathroom first." What will I say to them about Gray tonight? she thought. But she still couldn't believe that he wouldn't be back.

She had just got them settled down when a car drove in. It was Carrie Sears. She was a pretty woman who had always looked younger than her years, but today the prettiness had run all together somehow. She wore dark glasses and didn't take them off even in the house; her nose was red and her voice hoarse and unsteady.

"I don't know how to begin," she said, but she kept on talking. Gabbling, really. "I just wanted you to know I'm sorry about this . . . if I'd had any *idea*—the trouble I've had with that girl—willful—spoiled rotten—her father worships her . . ."

Astrid couldn't endure it. "Listen. Your daughter—" she still couldn't say the name—"is seventeen, but my husband's twenty-eight. You don't have anything to apologize to me about. Just let's hope it blows over, and—"

"But do you think I'd have let her come and babysit here, with him bringing her home, if I'd thought anything was going on?"

"No, I don't," Astrid assured her.

"Rupe's like you, he says she'll be back. That Gray'll bring her back. But it's like Rupe's stunned. He can't move. I couldn't sit there and watch him stare into space. He won't even watch TV," she added incredulously. The blotches deepened on her face and her hands shook.

"Would you like a cup of tea?" Astrid asked her.

"Yes," she said eagerly. "How can you be so cool?"

"I have to keep cool because of the children."

Carrie lowered her voice. "Oh, those poor little tykes. So innocent. She's always been a trouble. Oh, she puts on a great appearance. Knows how to carry herself, how to be nice, show good manners in public. Like Rupe's family that way. A bigger gang of street angels and house devils you'll never meet. It's been a fight almost since the day she was born. I never thought we'd raise her this far. I thought she'd be killed in an accident, always driving some boy's car with no license, and trying out everything that came along, like beer and pot, and I'd hate to think what else. Well, she seemed to turn over a new leaf this winter, and I thought it was Kevin made all the difference, she'd fallen for a *nice* boy at last. Well! We drew the biggest breath of relief, both of us. And then it turns out he was just the go-between."

"*What?*"

Carrie nodded solemnly. "She threw that in our faces last night. Did you ever check if Gray was really playing poker with the volunteer firemen or playing cribbage somewhere? We thought we were sending her out with Kevin to a basketball game or a wingding at some other kid's house. Then he'd bring her home again. It turns my stomach the way she'd sparkle all over the place and act like Kevin was her best beau. . . . He used to blush a lot," she added, more quietly. "Maybe we should give him credit for that."

If she doesn't go pretty soon I may just strangle her, Astrid thought. Instead she poured more tea.

They both drank thirstily, as if they were dehydrated.

"I never *guessed*," Carrie went on with new energy, "till Laura Manning came over yesterday and said she wanted to talk to me, and she hoped I wouldn't get mad. Seems Dorri's been bragging to the other kids for months about this married man and how they were carrying on right under his wife's nose." She turned dark red. "Excuse me, Astrid, but I have to say it like it was. Roxie told her mother finally, but Laura thought it was just some of Dorri's yarns—she's always been quite a liar—till yesterday. She picked up the telephone and Roxie was on the extension, and Dorri was telling her to say Gray had brought her around to leave a book the night before, in case anybody asked.... Laura never let on she heard, but she came over to see me. Are you all right, Astrid? You're an awful funny color."

"I'm all right." Gray had lied about that, then. They'd never been near the Mannings'. There was a disgusting, demeaning satisfaction in hearing it all, like gobbling cheap chocolates that were making you sick, but you couldn't help taking another one.

"Well, I was ready when Miss Lady came home last night from wherever she *said* she was all afternoon," Carrie said.

But Gray was on the job all afternoon, Astrid thought, and when he came home, he was affectionate, even demonstrative. Joking about the May basket—the memory impaled her. She'd thought he was relieved and happy because she was willing for him to make a change and because he'd made up his mind to act quickly. Had the relief been because of another decision, the special tenderness for her because he was clearing his conscience? Why, then, did he have to run to *her* when she summoned him?

The appalling incredulity hit her again, like the head-on crash at the brim of the fog-filled hollow. Carrie's voice ran monotonously on, as if it had been running for hours. "She threw him in our faces. Bragged how he'd get her anything she wanted, he loved her and she loved him— you never heard such carryings-on. Of course we lit into her, and she gave us a lot of four-letter words and tore out. Walked clear to the Mannings', but Laura wouldn't let her use the phone to call Gray, so she rampsed out of there, and all evening we kept looking for her to come back." Carrie took a long noisy swallow of tea. "Then she called up about midnight and says, in that hifalutin' way she can put on—" Carrie's imitation was uncannily true; their voices were somewhat alike—" 'I thought you'd like to know Gray's left his wife for me, and we're together now for good.' Slam goes the telephone. Well, I thought Rupe was going to have a stroke. He's nothing like the rest of the Searses or he'd have given her a good goin' over the night before. I had to get a couple of stiff drinks into him to lay him out. I took another tranquilizer."

Astrid spoke carefully because her voice wasn't reliable. "Carrie, whatever craziness this all is, I think Gray was ready to put an end to it. So right now maybe he's trying to wind things up."

"They've been together all night," Carrie said shrewdly.

"They could have been fighting all night. He's been disturbed about some other things that could have made him go in for this the way some men might take to drink." But was it really the firm? Maybe it had been Dorri all the time. Suddenly she couldn't say any more. She stared into her teacup, idly stirring, and Carrie pushed back her chair. "You're bushed. Look, I'll call you if I hear anything and you call me, okay?" She reached over and clumsily patted Astrid's shoulder. "Maybe you're right and it'll all blow over. One thing about nowadays, there's always some new scandal coming along to make folks forget the last one."

Astrid went to the door with her. "Thanks for coming, Carrie. I'm awfully sorry about everything."

"Good God, *you're* not to blame. Who'd ever expect this of a Price?" She laughed hoarsely. "This'll bring St. Fletcher flopping down to earth like an old pair of pants."

Astrid felt a twinge of anger, but she was too worn out to defend him. Besides, he didn't need it. She watched Carrie go and then went in to lie on the sofa. But she couldn't; this was where Gray had spent the last two nights wrestling with his conscience. Or with lust, she thought cynically. Carrie's visit had shaken her out of that sick, fumbling shock, and now she felt almost clearheaded with outrage and furious humiliation. If the two stood before her now, it would be a toss-up which one she would want to strangle first.

# Chapter
# 4

She lay on the floor finally with a cushion under her head, trying to breathe deeply, and was just starting to feel floaty when the boys came down the stairs talking to each other. She shut her eyes. One thing was certain: night must come.

"Now you stand right there," Peter commanded. "And when I say Jump, you must jump, and then I'll say what I'm s'poze to say."

She sat up, hoping Peter hadn't stationed the always obliging Chris halfway up the stairs. Anything was possible now; maybe Peter secretly wanted to do away with his little brother. But before she was on her feet Peter said, "Jump!" There was a small thud and a giggle, and then Peter said theatrically, "*Oh! Father* is *dying* on his *birthday!*"

She stood in the doorway and they looked around at her with faces as innocent as flowers. "Did you hear our play?" Peter asked.

"Yes. What happens next?"

"That's the end. I'll think up another one tomorrow. Can we have milkncookies?"

"There will always be milkncookies," she told them. Even if Father keeps dying on his birthday and leaving me with all the lies to tell. *Oh, Gray!* she almost cried aloud on a great wave of pain.

They had milk and cookies at the kitchen table, and she drank more tea, scalding all the way down. Someone knocked on the back door and the children were all bright expectation. Peter sang out "Come in!" before she could.

"Hello, men." But Kevin kept his eyes on Astrid. The blush flooded up his neck and into his face; the rims of his ears were fiery. His Adam's apple jumped as he swallowed. "I'm sorry," he said.

She moved her head toward the children, and he glanced at them quickly and then away, as if their puppyish trust was too much for him. "I have to explain something," he said.

"Everybody has to explain something, it seems." Except the Belle of the Ball, who just tells everyone how it's going to be. "So you might as well, even if I don't want to hear it. Make it quick, with no names."

"I thought it was all *her*. I mean, like she was making up these things the way she does. Like the math teacher was crazy about her, and the reason he wouldn't give her a passing mark was because she wouldn't come across. Well, nobody believed that. So I thought it was more of the same; she had a crush and any day now he'd tell her she was a pest and to split, or he'd tell her father. And I'd be there, see?" His eyes went shiny. "I'd be the *real* one that she wouldn't have to make up lies about." He laced his big hands together and began cracking his knuckles; the boys stared at his fingers as if hypnotized.

"Then I came to. He *was* in it." His voice broke. "We had a hell of a fight. But afterwards ... well, it was a choice of seeing her or never seeing her, and I kept hoping it would fall apart. I couldn't believe Gr— he could be *serious*. Married to *you*." If possible he was a deeper scarlet than before.

"All right, Kevin," she said. "You don't have to say any more." Peter's head had begun to swing alertly from one to the other.

"But I've been feeling so damn guilty."

"Is that why you came around yesterday? You didn't look very happy."

"I wasn't. She'd been on the phone yesterday morning bragging how she was calling the shots. I thought if he was here I'd tell him something. I'd tell him what she's really like, if I had to."

"But he wasn't here."

"Nope, and I couldn't say it to you, could I?"

He was imploring, and she said, "No, you couldn't."

"Well, she called me this morning and said she'd done it. I called her something and she laughed like hell and hung up. And, Astrid, she can be so damn sweet," he said desperately, "you'd never believe she could be anything else!" He looked about to cry.

She said hastily, "How about a good hot cup of tea, Kevin? It's been keeping me going on the longest day of my life."

"Are you sick, Kevin?" Peter asked.

"I've got an awful headache, chum. Played too much baseball yesterday, I guess." He rubbed his eyes.

"Daddy's going to take us to the ball game someday."

"Why don't you boys go out and play with your trucks while Kevin has an aspirin and some tea?" Astrid suggested.

"Will you come out after you drink your tea?" Peter asked him.

"I sure will." Kevin rumpled their heads. They went happily out.

She got aspirin for him and some fresh tea. "Have you eaten anything today?"

"Not much."

"Neither have I. How about some crackers and cheese? Keep me company."

"All right." He was eager to be of use.

"But I don't want to talk about it any more," she told him. "It'll be over soon, and the less there's been said, the better."

"*I'll* never say anything," he said gloomily, "but *she's* been scattering bulletins from hell to breakfast. She's a telephone addict."

"Never mind." She was firm.

The telephone rang. They both looked aghast at it. "If it's Dorri, hang up on her," he said hoarsely.

It was Gray. "I'm calling from the booth outside the store," he said. "Is there anybody else there? I want to see you."

"There won't be anyone else here."

"Then I'm on my way." He hung up. She tried to keep her face straight, not knowing whether it would laugh or cry.

"Kevin, will you take the boys for a long walk out

around the point? Finish your tea first. You've got a few minutes before he gets here."

"If it's Gray, I don't want to see him." He almost kicked his chair over. "How long do you want me to be gone with the kids?"

"Oh, an hour or so. That should be enough. They love to meander, so let them take their time, and I'll be forever obliged."

"Listen, *anything* I can do," he said fervently. She gave him extra sweaters for the boys and he loped out, happy to be doing something. "Hey, men!" he yelled. "How about a long hike?"

"Yeah!" Peter yelled back, and Chris flung up both arms and piped an echo. Kevin tucked him up on one arm, took Peter by the other hand, and went off out of sight around the barn.

Astrid ran upstairs and looked nervously into her mirror. Her slacks and blue shirt were neat. She gave her hair another brushing and tied it back with a blue scarf knotted at the nape. Her eyes were slightly bloodshot and stary, but she looked all together and that was important when she remembered the abject heap Gray had left on the sofa this morning. She put on fresh lipstick, went in and straightened the boys' beds, went down the back way to the kitchen and was gathering up the glasses and teacups when Gray stopped the pick-up behind Kevin's car. He stood looking at this, then came on into the house, frowning.

"I thought you said you were alone."

"I am. I asked Kevin to take the boys for a walk." She was proud of her easy manner.

"What's *he* doing around here?"

Her easy manner almost departed. But he's not my enemy; he's my husband and I love him, she reminded herself.

"He stopped by to see if there was anything he could do, and there was. So he's doing it." She put her clammy hands in her pockets. He ran his through his hair, looked around the kitchen as if he had been away for a long time.

"We have to talk," he began.

"Gray, if you're back we don't have to talk about it."

"I'm not back."

She moved cautiously sidewise to a chair, sat down and folded her arms on the table. "Why not?"

"They threw her out; she's got nowhere to go!" he said angrily. "So it's up to me to take care of her, and I want to. I'm in love with her. It's not that I don't love *you*, but this is different. It's like something terminal, that I can't get over no matter how I try. I'm sorry."

"You're not sorry, or you wouldn't be in this mess," she said. "Nothing on earth could make you walk out on your family for a sexy kid unless you really wanted to."

He flushed. "You make me sound like a child-molester! She's seventeen and mature for her age. My mother was married at sixteen."

"To another sixteen-year-old," she retorted. "And you may be interested to know that your girl friend wasn't thrown out, she walked out, and her father almost worried himself into the hospital wondering where she was."

"I made her call them."

"That was great of you, considering that you were contributing to the delinquency of their minor child."

The flush faded, leaving a grayish cast. He braced his

hands on the back of a chair, but before he could speak she added, "I said 'contributing to.' She was already a delinquent."

"I didn't come here to hear her attacked!"

"Gracious! It's good you weren't here earlier. There's been quite a bit of testimony offered to prove you were right when you told me she wasn't quite the little innocent I thought. In fact she's a nasty little piece of work."

"Kevin's so jealous he can't see straight."

"It was her mother who talked the most. Kevin just came to apologize for being the go-between. Gray, I guess I know why you objected to Kevin keeping her company here. *You* were the jealous one. Never mind about what Peter might see, you were writhing with jealousy the whole time. And I thought it was the firm!"

"It *was* the firm. It's been depressing me for a long time, I swear it. This other thing—I never intended for it to happen, but I was feeling so damn low one night when I took her home, and suddenly—well, it started in all innocence."

"Oh, Gray, stop it! Nothing like that starts in all innocence." Her throat closed up and clogged with tears; they filled her eyes. She said thickly, "I can't stand talking to you like this! I love you! Gray, I don't care how it started or how far it went." She had to stop and blow her nose. "Come back now. Be here when the kids get home, and stay, and we'll never mention it again."

"I can't. She's waiting in that motel for me."

And calling everybody she knows, Astrid thought. "Tell Rupe and Carrie where she is, let them go and get her. This can be forgotten in a couple of weeks." If you haven't got her pregnant, she added in silence.

His face was stolid. "I came for some clothes and to leave you some money. When I get settled I'll give you my address—for the divorce."

He counted the bills out on the table. She watched without moving until he had finished, and then she picked them up and handed them to him. "You'll need every cent, if only to pay for her telephone calls." A perilous hilarity was trying to take over, and the thought of having hysterics frightened her, "Go away," she said, "before the children come back."

"What are you telling them about me?"

"By rights I should let you think up the story and do the telling. It ought to be good." That manic laughter was going to seize her in another instant. "It would be so simple if I could just say Father has died on his birthday."

"*What?*"

She spun away from him before he could see her face break up, and the physical action helped. She fixed her gaze on the blue cove down there. "Gray, if you're not back to stay, get your clothes and go *now*. No more talk."

"To hell with the clothes!" he shouted and slammed out of the house. She stood staring at the tender blues and greens all swimming and melting together in her vision, until the sound of the truck died away. The threat of hysteria died with it, leaving her cold and weak as if she'd gotten up too soon from the flu. She turned back to the room. The bills lay scattered across a bright braided rug.

If I lived alone, she thought, I'd leave them there till they rotted. She gave in to a profane energizing gust of rage, knowing it would stave off the tears. When the kids were asleep that night she could let go.

Kevin was plainly disappointed. "I got to thinking some-body'd come back. You know. Thought better of it. It's so *crazy*, Astrid. To give up everything..." He nodded at her and then at the children spreading out their loot on the back steps.

"I don't know if that's happened, Kevin. Nobody's thinking straight right now, least of all him."

"You can say that again. I'll go now. You look dead on your feet."

"Thanks for walking the boys."

"Listen, Astrid, I'll do anything. You know that. Baby-sit, mow the lawn, fix something—you just call on me, will you?"

He was so eager that she promised him, not expecting ever to take him up on it. She was glad he'd been around to keep the boys out, but she could never forget he'd been a part of the conspiracy; he'd seen Gray as Dorri's lover and had heard Dorri laughing at her. Now he wanted to get the guilt off his back, and who else should receive the burden but her?

"And keep your doors locked at night," he was telling her. "You got a phone beside your bed? In case those Cades try to raise hell with you?"

"I'll call somebody if they show up," she promised.

"Call *me!*" he said, but she laughed. "No, I'll call George Rollins or the sheriff's patrol."

"All right," he said grumpily and left.

Now she could get the boys into the tub and then into their pajamas. Chris was very sleepy. Peter was busy talk-ing about the seals they'd seen, his sea urchin, the big blue mussel shells, traps wound up in rockweed, part of a wrecked skiff, until in the middle of supper he said all at once, "Where's Daddy?"

"Oh, Daddy called," she said. "He has to go away on business. Some daddies have to do that, you know. He sent you his love."

She hoped the glib excuse would slide over everything, but Peter said, "What kind of business? Is he going to build a house for somebody?"

"I think probably."

"Is Uncle Fletch and Uncle Cam going too?"

"No."

"Is he going to build the house all by himself?"

"He could. He's a very fine carpenter."

"That's what I'm going to be." He went on eating his cheese sandwich. She thought, Well, that's over with for the night.

Chris was ready for bed, but Peter wasn't. "Can't we have some songs first?"

She tried to dissuade him, but he had his second wind and was keyed up. She put Chris to bed, and when she came downstairs Peter had already gotten out the worn old book *Baby's Opera*, with her grandmother's name written in it. He had it up on the music rack and open to the first song.

"Peter, we can't do them all," she said firmly. "For one thing, I'm just too tired. So we'll do three."

He knew the tone and accepted it, but he had a hard time making up his mind, so she made it up for him. She suggested two titles and then he demanded "The Frog and the Crow."

"All right, but only one verse," she said.

She was never a pianist. Her parents had given up early

on that, because she had simply been leaden at her lessons until she defeated them; but she could read music and play simple things well enough for the children's pleasure.

She felt lightheaded with fatigue when she had at last tucked him in, and thought she would pass out with no difficulty in her own bed. But it was Gray's bed as well. She went into the spare room, but that was no better; now everything came down on her like an avalanche. Dorri laughing; Dorri giggling with her friends about her; Dorri in Gray's arms. This was intolerable—unthinkable—and yet it had happened. In a motel somewhere, Graham Price, her Gray, was probably naked in bed with the seventeen-year-old babysitter. The thought brought her out of her own bed, wanting to find them, to rip them apart, to punch and to slap until noses bled and lips split—

*Oh God, oh God!* she heard herself saying. It was just a sound to make, like a howl or a moan. If she were as truly devout as Fletch and Nora, she could find some comfort in prayer or in reading her Bible, she supposed; but she was a pagan in agony.

She walked through the house; she went outdoors in bathrobe and bare feet and walked on the cold wet grass until she was completely chilled. Back in the spare-room bed, she finally fell into a sleep so heavy that when she woke up it was like coming out of anesthesia—she kept dropping back into it, giving in for a little, and then realized the children would be waking soon. She fought all the way up. She remembered before full consciousness that something terrible had happened; and when she was completely awake the remembrance was complete too.

He had said "Divorce."

# Chapter 5

**B**ut the heavy sleep had helped. She felt stronger, less in danger of flying apart into a few thousand irretrievable fragments. The shock of disbelief was less. It had happened, but all she had to do was to keep imagining how it would be this morning if he had died yesterday; just to know that he was still alive was a relief. This would work as long as she could keep from biting down on the raw nerve of Dorri standing there by the kitchen table two nights ago, gushing admiration. Then the jaunty bit over her shoulder on the way out: "He's never cheated me yet!"

Her laughter had not been with Astrid, but *at* her; how soon before they were in each other's arms? *That girl in Gray's arms.* And where had they parked for that lost hour? He'd been trying to break off with her, he said. Astrid could hardly believe that now. She could only believe that she did not know this man who had lied so glibly to her for so long. He was not her Gray; he was a changeling.

She changed the beds and did a washing. She rearranged

the spare room for herself. Then she went out to look for dandelion greens in the field. Whenever the boys found an early blossom they held it under each other's chin or under hers and demanded, "Do you like butter?" Swallows and gulls performed. Two lobster boats came into the cove to set traps, and the boys were enthralled, waving excitedly. The men waved back, and she wondered if they had heard anything yet.

"Maybe I'll be a lobsterman," Peter said.

"Me too," said Chris, the echo.

"I thought you wanted to be a carpenter," Astrid said.

"I can catch lobsters too. Uncle Ben says I can be his helper. I can do that when me and Daddy aren't building a house."

"I see. Don't pick the little white flowers, Chris. They'll be strawberries by and by." Chris looked skeptical, but desisted.

There was a shrill whistle from across the field. Dinah Neville was coming around the barn, her woolly mongrel terrier plunging ahead of her. The children screamed exultantly, "Here, Poochie, Poochie! Hi, Poochie!"

He arrived like a projectile and all three went into an ecstatic heap in the grass, a panting, giggling tangle of legs and a wildly wagging tail. Dinah was Astrid's oldest friend in town, dating from the time when Astrid's parents first bought the place from Dinah's grandfather for a summer home. Dinah had lived in the next cove then, and she and Astrid, twelve-year-olds, traveled back and forth by bicycle on the road, on foot through the woods, or by skiff around the point. Now she lived at the harbor; she'd married earlier than Astrid—she and Ben having anticipated too fervently while in the last year of high school—so her children were in school now.

"Finding any greens this early?" she asked. She was tall and leggy in jeans and turtleneck, lightly freckled, her brown hair tied back at the nape of her neck. Her large glasses customarily slid down an aquiline nose and she was always looking over them. She looked over them at Astrid now and said, "If your mother could see you at this moment, she'd disown you. She's always so elegant. I used to think she should be called Madame instead of plain Mrs."

"She thinks so too. Maybe that's why she goes to France so much. And I know she stays away from here so she won't see me on my knees digging dandelion greens like a peasant, or bottoms up in the clam flats, or chopping firewood."

Dinah sat down beside her in the grass. The boys ran through the field with the dog; the laughing and the barking joined the cries of gulls and quarreling of swallows. Astrid watched with instinctive pleasure until reality struck her again. Her sight blurred, and she took a long shaky breath. She realized that Dinah was watching her and not the children and dog.

"I heard something really weird yesterday." It was not like Dinah to sound so shy. "I don't believe it, but I don't know how it started, unless that rotten kid started it herself, for kicks."

"You heard that Gray's left me," said Astrid, staring straight ahead. "Well, he has. For the rotten kid."

"Oh, my God!" whispered Dinah. "Astrid, *no!* Not Graham Price!"

Astrid nodded, still not able to look at her.

"If that little slut can get Gray, I'm going to chain Ben and me together." She seized Astrid's arm and shook it. "What's *happened* to him? Is he having a nervous break-down?"

"I'd love to believe that. Maybe this is what he's doing instead of having one."

"What's he got to have a nervous breakdown *for?*" Dinah scoffed. "No, I take that back. Give him a couple of weeks with Little Hot Pants and he'll be ready for the booby hatch. Oh, my gosh, Astrid, I shouldn't talk like that, but I'm so shook up I'm going to explode. *Gray!*"

"It's okay, Dine. You can talk. How did you find out?"

"My kid sister told me that Dorri—if I can say her name without upchucking—was calling up all these kids and say-ing she'd forced her married man to leave his wife, and it was Gray Price, and they were staying in a fancy motel up near Belfast. And he'd gone to tell his wife he wanted a divorce. Now this came to Sandy through Dorri's side-kick Mavis Carter, and we all know what *she* is. So I told Sandy to consider the source. She couldn't believe the yarn anyway." Dinah's eyes were wide with shock. "Oh, Astrid!"

"Dorri told me once," said Astrid dryly, "that she knew Mavis had gotten off to a wrong start in life, but she was trying to help her to straighten out."

"Yeah? Well, at least Mavis's trips into the puckerbrush are with boys her own age. Astrid, *has* Gray been back? Did he mention divorce?"

Astrid nodded. Having to talk about it, even with some-one as close as Dinah, was only reviving the horror with transfusions of fresh blood.

"So what are you going to do?"

"Nothing but wait. I'm not the one who wants to get married. I'm already married. To Gray." As she said it, everything became marvelously and soothingly lucid. There was nothing she had to do but wait.

"Hurray for you!" Dinah shouted. "I've been worried sick since yesterday, not wanting to come barging right around to ask you. Oh, hey, I drove around by the new house on the way here, and Gray was up on the roof with his back to me, but Cam was full of blarney as usual, and Fletch was all right. So they hadn't heard anything."

"That won't last for long. Nora will know as soon as Hugh gets off the school bus this afternoon."

"I think I'll go back to the new house on my way home," said Dinah, "and tell Gray I'd like a word alone with him."

"Dinah, don't!" Astrid exclaimed in real alarm. "*Please!*"

"Then I'll set Ben on him. He'll be feather-white when he hears the truth. He thought Dorri made up this yarn because she'd probably made a pass at Gray sometime and he'd told her off. He said Gray was lucky she hadn't accused him of rape."

"Look, Dinah, I know you and Ben are loyal, and I don't know what I'd do without you. But when I said I wasn't going to do anything but wait, I meant it, and I don't want anybody else to do anything, either. There'll be a big argument with Fletch and Cam about it, but please don't make me argue with *you*."

"I'd never have believed you'd be this all together," Dinah said. "I mean, I've seen you scared silly an awful lot of times ever since we were twelve. But now look at you, when there's really something to worry about."

"I'm not that much all together, Dinah, except maybe

the way glass is. One long high note and I could shatter. Let's have a cup of coffee. Whistle to the boys. I can't do it the way you can."

"It's so easy. You just take your two fingers like this, see?" She demonstrated, with instant results. Astrid laughed. They walked toward the house hand in hand as they had done as children.

Dinah stayed for lunch, and they talked about the summer activities ahead as if life were going on as usual for Astrid. It was like talking fantasy, but quite simple once you got the hang of it.

After Dinah left, promising to keep her righteous indignation within bounds, Astrid settled the boys for their naps, promising that they would have a dog like Poochie when Chris got to be four years old. "How can I stand to wait that long?" Peter asked.

"We all have to wait a long time sometimes for something we want. You can learn to row while you're waiting."

Chris immediately bounced up. "Me too?"

"Not till you're four, Chris," said Peter in his deepest voice. "When do I start, Mama?"

"When it's summer. And it'll be summer after the garden's all in. Then we'll get the skiff out for you. . . . If you have a good nap we'll go for a walk when you get up. Or we can work on the dory."

"All right." They squeezed their eyes shut.

She was cleaning the few greens on the back doorstep when Carrie called.

"And how are you, dear?" she asked in a hushed tone suitable for addressing the bereaved.

"All right, thanks," said Astrid briskly.

"And how are the little fellers?"

"Having their naps."

"What do they think of all this, poor little tykes?"

"They don't know anything about it. Is Rupert all right, Carrie?"

"Ayuh. The reason I called . . ." All at once she became stridently businesslike. "The reason I called is that the way things are working out, we've decided not to swear out any complaint against Gray." She waited while the echoes clanged against Astrid's eardrums. She couldn't say anything, so Carrie went on. "They told us at the barracks that they won't bring back runaways like Dorri unless she's committed some crime or there's a complaint against *him*, like statu—something or other—*rape*—" she bore down hard on that one—"which is hard to prove. Or contributing to the delinquency of a minor. Well, we could do that all right, and lug her home, and he'd be put under bond not to see her. I *think* I've got it straight what they told us. But it would be pure hell around here. We'd have to keep her locked in her room, and we can't do that. Whenever Dorri wants something, she *never* lets up. She's some persistent!" she finished proudly. "You still there, Astrid?"

"Yes." Why don't I hang up on her? But she could not.

"Rupe thinks too much of the Prices to want to raise a stink against them. So when she called us this morning from school—"

"You mean she's still going to school?" For some reason it was ridiculous.

"Oh yes!" Carrie sounded affronted. "What do you *think?* He wants her to finish her education."

Astrid found this even more ridiculous, or else hysteria

was threatening again. She could think of many things to say, but was able to hold back while Carrie went on. "So when she told us this morning that everything's all set, he's been and talked to you and you've agreed to a divorce and all, well, that just made up our minds for us." She was complacent, if not actually jaunty. "And it's very nice of you, Astrid. We really appreciate it!"

"But I never agreed to a divorce," Astrid said.

There was silence at the other end. Then Carrie asked weakly, "But wasn't he there? Yesterday afternoon?"

"Divorce was never discussed." *Not by me, anyway.*

"I can't figure this out!" Carrie bleated. "She *told* me! And she was some happy! She's so in love—she wants everything right and nice . . ."

*And I'm spoiling it for her, mean old me. Is that what you mean?* "*I'm* not a liar, Carrie," she said calmly. "And as far as raising a stink, it's already been done. Now I think this conversation's gone far enough." She hung up and stood there trembling with fury. She felt filthy from having been forced to talk about her private affairs with this woman.

*Calm down, calm down,* she told herself. *This woman is only poor nitwit Carrie Sears. Dorri must have been putting her and Rupe through hoops, flaming ones, for years. No wonder she's drunk with the hope of getting rid of her and to such a fantastic catch.*

# Chapter
# 6

Tonight she would pack a picnic supper and take the boys far around the shore somewhere and stay out until it was time to put them to bed. She'd take a long warm bath and go to bed herself with the telephone off the hook. Tomorrow they'd go away for the day, maybe to Pemaquid.

She finished the greens and left them in a pail of cold water and was washing her hands when the telephone rang again. She set out to let it ring, then decided to answer; she could always hang up if she didn't like what was at the other end.

"*There* you are!" It was Nora. "I was worried. Are you all right?"

"Why shouldn't I be all right, Nora? What have you heard?"

For once Nora was out of words, and Astrid said gently, "You might as well get it over with." Nora held her strong voice down with an effort. "Hugh just got home from school; he told us what he'd heard and I told him he was crazy, or somebody was. But he swore Gray dropped Dorri off at school this morning."

"Gray to work and Dorri to school—Carrie's *so* pleased!"

"Are you laughing, Astrid? Or crying? I'm coming right over there!"

"No, you aren't, Nora. The boys will be up in a few minutes, and I won't say anything in front of them. But I can guess what Hugh heard, and most of it's true, I guess."

After a moment Nora said, almost inaudibly, "I can't really take it in. If he's on the job I wonder if he's told Fletch. Oh, dear, I hate to be the one."

"Let Hugh do it," said Astrid.

"Listen, he's already skinned out of the house to dig clams, and if I know him he'll wangle a supper invitation somewhere and call up later to see if he can stay all night. I threatened him with battle, murder, and sudden death if I ever heard he'd been talking about this to anybody. Look, Fletch and I'll be over by and by."

"All right, but don't make it until after seven. I want to be sure the boys are asleep." When she hung up and turned away, Peter was at the foot of the back stairs.

"Was that Daddy?"

"No, it was Aunt Nora."

He sat down hard on the bottom step, ready to burst into tears. "I wish he wouldn't build old houses! I wish he'd come *home!* I *miss* him!"

Before her own tears could strike, she took him into her arms. "I do too, darling," she said, "but we can do nice things while we're waiting. We can get the dory ready. How about that? And tonight we'll have a picnic."

"Oh boy!" He brightened. "Can I go wake up Chris?"

"No, let's give him a few more minutes. You know how tired he gets."

"He's younger than me," said Peter importantly.

Fletch and Nora arrived about half past seven. Nora was a big woman, too firm-fleshed and immaculate to be called blowsy. She gathered Astrid into a hard hug, patting her on the back, and then released her and said briskly, "*Well!*"

Fletch, not usually demonstrative, held her hand and looked searchingly into her face with his dark Price eyes, so like Gray's and yet unlike. "Are you all right, Astrid?" he asked her. She knew what Fletch meant by *all right*.

"I'm living one hour at a time, Fletch, the best the boys and I can do."

"Good girl," he said gruffly.

"Come on into the living room," she said. "Would anyone want tea or coffee?" She knew better than to offer them drinks.

"Not now," Fletch said. "Let's get this over with."

She told it as briefly as possible. "I *never!*" Nora exclaimed at intervals. Fletch kept taking off his glasses to wipe them, a sign of his distress, though he was controlled in his manner and speech. His older-brother concern for Astrid seemed to strengthen her; one of the worst things about this situation was her constant fear of suddenly going to pieces without warning.

When she finished, Nora said, "He's gone crazy. That's what it is. Just like that great-uncle of yours, Fletch, the one your folks never wanted to talk about."

"We don't have to talk about him now," said Fletch patiently. "And I'm not trying to hide the poor old sinner. We're concerned with Graham. To think he came to work today straight from this—this . . ." He struggled but couldn't find, or wouldn't use, the word he wanted. "And went back to it tonight. He could look Cam and me in the face without a quiver of conscience! . . . He didn't have an awful lot to say, but he takes spells like that; we all do. So I didn't give it much mind."

He paced the room. "He's not crazy, he is *evil*. As evil as these boys rampaging up and down the roads, destroying for the sake of destruction."

"They vandalized Simmy Tolliver's house last night while he was at church," Nora said to Astrid. "Because he put one of the younger ones off the school bus for using foul language. We all know it's the Cades, but if you can't catch them in the act, and you can't say anything to their father . . ." She shrugged. "It'll be vigilantes next, you wait and see. It'll have to be."

"My brother's an adulterer," said Fletch quietly. "Breaking the commandments, going against everything decent, shattering the lives of his wife and children. He's no different from those boys, but they were brought up to be what they are. He wasn't. It makes him doubly evil."

"*No!*" Astrid protested, and Nora said, "Fletch, you know Gray's not bad. It has to be something else, like a sickness."

*Like something terminal*, Gray said, *that I can't get over*.

Astrid was glad to see Cam's car drive in. She jumped up to meet him and Harriet at the door. Harriet was primly pretty and showed a faint resemblance to Carrie Sears, who was a cousin. Cam always greeted Astrid with a kiss and did so tonight, saying tenderly, "How are you, kid?" Unexpectedly, Harriet kissed her too.

"If I'd known the facts this morning," Cam said violently, "I'd have taken him by the scruff of the neck and shaken him shitless."

"Watch your language, Cameron," Fletch reproved him.

"I know you're not the cold fish you sound like," Cam retorted. "But why don't you give in once and show a little righteous rage? This calls for more than prayer, brother. So let's hear something constructive from the amen corner."

"I want to talk with him," said Fletch. "I want him to tell me himself what he's done and why. Then I'll try to reason with him. I'll give him every chance, Astrid, never fear. But if he persists in this evil, I'll give him his notice, and he can find another way to support his—this girl. We'll pay his salary to you and the boys."

Harriet said suddenly, "Rupe and Carrie need their heads knocked together. They've been letting that girl do as she pleased since she took her first step. No wonder she's out of control now."

"But that doesn't excuse Gray's going out of control," said Fletch. "She's a child still, according to the law. Gray could be arrested any time her parents choose. That'll be the next thing," he said grimly. "As soon as Rupe gets his breath."

"No," said Astrid. "I think Gray's looking pretty good to them right now. They're expecting him to marry her, so they're not going to do anything." She held up her hands to silence their reactions. "I know he's your brother, and you've always been close, and you have family rights. But the boys and I are the ones he walked out on. I've had to do a lot of thinking since five o'clock yesterday morning. It feels like two years of thinking, instead of two days.

But what it comes down to is this: I can't believe he's going to throw all of us away because he thinks he's got this new, perfect life to live. I mean, give him a couple of weeks, and whatever he's feeling now—"

There was a ribald snort from Cam's corner.

"Whatever it is now, he can get over it in time. She's just a self-centered little kid who has but one aim in life, to get what *she* wants and to hell with everybody else. She's accomplished this, which means she could be tired of it in a few weeks. Unless Gray's got another, really extrovert, personality we don't know anything about—"

"He has," said Fletch.

"And it belongs in a padded cell," said Cam.

"Let her talk, you two!" said Nora. "She's making sense."

"What I mean is, Gray could be pretty dull for her after the new wears off. And he'll have got his head back, too."

"Especially if he feels guilty, and he misses the boys—and you too, dear," Nora assured her.

"So if none of us does anything, when he comes back it'll be that much easier for us to pick up and go on. Fletch," she said diffidently, "if he does his work all right, I wish you wouldn't fire him. I've got the checking account, and we have a joint savings account, so I'm all right. And, Cam, I know how *you* feel. There've been times in the last two days when I could've killed them both. But I have to take the long view. I just can't believe our life is ended."

They were quiet, looking at her with respect and affection. She felt like weeping with love; they had never been so much her own family.

"Well," said Fletch, looking at his pipe.

"How could you take him back, after this?" Harriet asked. "A motel with that girl, and all the cheap talk she's already made—"

"It's not going to be easy," Astrid said honestly. "I'll have to take each thing as it comes. I'm not being Christian," she said to Fletch. "I'm being selfish. He belongs to the boys and me."

"But wait a minute," Nora said. "What was that about them expecting him to marry her?"

"Oh, *that*." Astrid was having one of those rare moments of feeling on top of things. "Dorri told her mother that I'd agreed to a divorce. I told her I hadn't."

"What if he really pushes for one?"

She shook her head. "I'm not divorcing him."

"She may get pregnant just to force you," Harriet warned. "She's not used to being opposed."

"So her mother keeps telling me," Astrid said dryly. "Well, that's her problem, isn't it?"

"It's going to be a hell of a strain, keeping my mouth shut," said Cam.

"Yes, it is," said Harriet sweetly.

After that they were ready to eat. It turned out that nobody had wanted much supper in the first shock of finding out what had happened. Now they had a light meal together, and Astrid began to feel more like herself. But when they were gone and the house was silent again, it was like the emptiness of a cemetery. She went upstairs and sat in the boys' room for a while, listening to their light breathing and small animallike stirrings. Fatigue began to drug her. She went into the spare room, but the action roused her again, and she tried to read, but she didn't know what she was reading. Gray's name seemed to have been resounding through her head for days now, like a maddening tone one can't escape because it's inside the brain.

When they were leaving Fletch had said to her with ironic humor, "If I don't preach at him, you don't mind if I pray a lot, do you?"

"I'll be grateful, Fletch. If anyone's prayers are ever answered, yours should be." Now she thought it would be good to pray—to *believe* in prayer, so that it comforted you. Which meant believing there was a Listener. Well, if there was, He simply listened, and people went on doing their foul or foolish deeds.

# Chapter
# 7

It was surprising how soon you became used to something you could hardly believe. Good weather held for the next week, and she planted the garden; she split up more firewood; she worked hard scraping the dory; she took the boys for long walks around the shore or through the woods. On Saturday she and Dinah took all the children on the Pemaquid trip she'd thought of earlier. Either Nora or Harriet called her every day, not asking for news but letting her know that they were thinking of her. With all her physical exercise and keeping up with the boys during the days, she was able to get a fairly decent night's sleep, though she woke before dawn.

She had Sunday dinner at Fletcher's, for the boys' sake, and a supper at Cam's. She drove the boys to Limerock for new shorts, sneakers, jerseys, and hamburgers. The day turned out to be extremely hot, and when they came home, Kevin was mowing the lawn. She'd been looking forward to a shower and to reading down on the beach while the children played with their boats, letting the peace and quiet of the shady little cove take her over. But

Kevin was so pleased to be doing something for her that she hadn't the heart to resent him.

She made him a big pitcher of iced tea, and they sat in the shade at the front of the house, while the boys rolled down the newly mown slope.

"You look better," he told her shyly.

"Will power," she told him. "So don't offer me any news, or you'll ruin all my good work. You know the kind of news I mean."

His grin was a poor effort. He was still suffering from guilt and probably would as long as she and Gray were apart. She said with forced vigor, "Well, anybody lucky enough to catch a Cade yet?"

"Elmer got picked up for speeding on Main Street in Williston, and he didn't have a muffler either, but he'll get off with a fine. The old man got nabbed with some short lobsters. But that'll be like his jacking deer; he'll just keep paying the money and doing it again. But Damon Cade— hey, I almost forgot that!" He cheered up considerably. "He and some other jerks were over at the dump firing at rats with handguns, and Floyd Watts drove in. They began showing off, firing as close to him as they dared, and a bullet ricocheted off a rock and nearly hit him. He cussed them out, and they threatened him and fired at the truck as he left. He stopped at the first house he came to and called the sheriff. The patrol came right along and stopped 'em when they came out of the dump road, but they'd stashed their pistols somewhere and swore that Floyd was either crazy or drunk. Well, everybody knew they were lying, but I'll bet that bunch could manage to get away with murder."

"I suppose they'll trip themselves up someday, but it's a long time coming."

"Yeah. Well, knocking over mailboxes and driving trucks through somebody's garden, even breaking windows and making a mess in somebody's house—it's all a lot different from showing off with guns. Somebody else could have a gun too, you know, and pick 'em off some night just like that!" He snapped his fingers. "And say they thought they were shooting at porcupines."

"It would be nice if they thought of that possibility themselves," said Astrid. "It might quiet them down a bit."

"Not them, they think they've got charmed lives. And why not?" They got quite a lot of conversation out of the subject. When Kevin finished the iced tea and left, reluctantly, it was too late to take the children to the shore. They were short-tempered with sleepiness. She got them bathed and into bed early, escaping the songs tonight but not a conversation about Daddy's progress on the house and when he would probably start for home.

She called both Harriet and Nora and told them she was going to bed early. Fletch came on and told her sadly that Gray had quit, after Fletch's fourth attempt to reason with him.

"Never mind, Fletch, you did your best," she said.

"It wasn't good enough. I didn't say what he wanted to hear. He wanted me to understand how it was with him, and I couldn't understand and said so. You'll get his salary, Astrid, and don't argue. And keep an eye on the bank statements."

"All right," she said meekly, but she didn't really believe Gray would abuse their joint accounts.

When she came out of the bathroom in her robe, in the dusk, a man was sitting at the kitchen table. She gasped in terror, and he said quickly, "It's me!" It was Gray. Still trembling, she turned on the light over the table.

"Couldn't you have knocked?" she asked in a shaky voice. She wasn't prepared for him; she felt almost nauseated.

"I did, but you were in the shower," he said reasonably.

"Why didn't you call first, then?"

"And have you tell me not to come?"

"Gray, all I want is for you to come home."

He sat back in the captain's chair and rested one ankle across the other knee. His new slacks were bright red. She leaned against the counter, tightening the sash of her robe, and looked at him. He was letting his hair grow; it seemed thicker and fluffier and fell across his forehead, and she wondered if Dorri played with it and styled it as if he were a life-sized boy doll. With cynical amusement, she noted the chain hung around his neck over the white turtleneck and the sunglasses clipped in the breast pocket of the bright tartan sports jacket. Last Christmas she had given him one in a much more subtle pattern and he had said it was very nice, but he had never worn it and always had an excuse when she suggested it. She'd thought then that it wasn't conservative enough for him.

"Maybe it wasn't bright enough," she said aloud.

"What?" He seemed startled.

"I guess Cam isn't the only dandy any more." He was Gray and yet he was not, this gaudy peacock of a man who was the lover of a young girl. "Well, *have* you come back?"

His eyes flickered as if at a threatened blow, then became too fixed. "I brought you some money."

"I don't want it, Gray. You must need it all."

"The boys are my responsibility. Take it for them."

"I suppose it salves your conscience," she said mildly. "They think you've gone away to build a house somewhere, but I can't keep that up forever."

"It's more or less true. I've quit Fletch, and I'm on my own. I've got a job building a big wing on a summer place at Partridge Point across the river, and there's a nice apartment over the garage we can live in rent-free for the length of the job. The way things are nowadays, they want someone living on the place until they get here."

"That must be my answer," she said. "You haven't come home."

"I'm not coming home," he said with maddening patience. "It's not home now."

The whole devastating situation broke over her like a drowning wave; it roared in her ears, blinded her, cut off her breath. She fought frantically to the surface, worked words out of her aching throat. "Gray, I can't stand the thought of you making love to her!" she blurted. "Don't you see, that's what's killing me? You and *her*—you and anyone—you're *mine!*"

The unfamiliar man in the unfamiliar outfit said sadly, "No. I tried to fight it, but it didn't work. She wouldn't give up, she knew best."

"Gray, what did I *do?*"

"It's not you, it's me. I'm to blame, I'm the one the lightning struck. It could have happened to *you*," he said, almost pleadingly. Was this how he had talked to Fletch?

"It did once," she said. "With you."

"Oh hell, Astrid!" He got up and roamed around, hands in pockets. "I can't expect you to know how it is with a man."

"Oh, but I can guess!" The humiliating weakness was gone; her pride came back stronger than ever. "Lightning struck, and happiness is a warm seventeen-year-old. I'm thinking of trying it. There are a lot of cute young boys around."

He was offended. "Don't make such talk. You're not the type."

"But it's all right if you *are* the type. Like Dorri. Calling everybody and gloating. Laughing at me. Do you and she laugh together about old Astrid? Have you told her everything, all our secrets?"

"Stop that!" His cheekbones went red, and he slapped his hand down on the table. "I don't talk about you! I never would! And as for her, I didn't come here to hear her put down. You've got a right to be bitter—"

"Thanks."

"But it's not like you to be malicious."

"I'm learning," she said. "Of course I didn't start as young as Dorri, but with a little practice I can progress from malicious to vicious."

"She told me everybody's against her, lying about her, and they've got to you, haven't they? Can't you believe me when I tell you she's sick about all this! She even cried about it, because you were always so nice to her. But she couldn't help herself."

"Lightning struck her too? You must have both been standing under the same tree."

"She's deep and she's sensitive!" he shouted at her.

"Shut up!" she hissed at him. "Do you want the children down here so you can tell them now you've left them forever?"

He flinched and looked upward. Then he went on in a low voice. "You should see the poetry she writes. She's so mature for her years you'd never believe it. She's a *woman*. These kids who aren't dry behind the ears mean nothing to her."

"Except when they come in handy like Kevin. It was damned cold-blooded the way you two used him. You should be ashamed, Gray."

"Well, I am," he admitted. "But he's young, he'll get over it."

"And I will too, I suppose."

"You deserve the best, Astrid," he said warmly. "And you'll find it."

"I can't believe this dialogue!" She threw up her hands. "It's absolutely awful. If I heard it on TV or read it in a book, I'd give up in disgust. Or *throw* up."

"I'm sorry if I make you feel like puking," he said with dignity. "I'm trying to be honest. I want a divorce. You wouldn't listen the other day."

"But I heard from Carrie that the divorce is all set, and she was about to become your mother-in-law. She was so happy about it I thought you were going to give her a diamond too."

"You'll have to ignore Carrie. She rattles on."

"But where did she ever get such an idea?" Astrid asked innocently. "Did *you* tell her it was a sure thing?"

He brushed that off. "How about it? I'm trying to be

honest, I told you, and fair. The sooner we settle it the better it will be for everybody. The kids'll accept the situation. They like Dorri—"

"Well, I don't! I did once. But with what I know about her now I wouldn't let the children get any closer to her than to a typhoid carrier. I don't know why I bother to tell you that. I'm not divorcing you, Gray. You haven't taken long enough to know what you really want, and I'm not about to join the Give-Dorri-what-she-wants-because-she-won't-shut-up-till-she-gets-it-Club."

"I'll call you," he said angrily and walked out.

She stood where she was, shivering and faint, listening to the pick-up driving out. She had believed that the worst thing would be to know that Gray was dead. Now she wasn't so sure. These terrible passions of rage, jealousy, grief, and longing, with which she had to deal, must be a hundred times worse. There wasn't enough of her to withstand them. They'll kill me, she thought, and *he'll* go on with Dorri—they'll have the children.

This snapped her out of the frightening mood. She became aware that Peter was calling her, and she went up to him. He was sitting up in bed, his eyes big. "I heard Daddy's voice," he whispered. "Is he home?"

She sat beside him and hugged him to her. "It must have been a dream."

"Did he drive away again? I heard the truck!"

"Darling, it was a dream, I told you."

"No," he protested. He was trying not to cry. Chris was fussing tearfully in his sleep, and this wasn't natural. She went on stroking Peter's rigid back, felt him fighting his tears, and then give in to quiet sobbing against her shoulder. Too quiet, too sad for a small boy.

I could kill you for this, Gray, she thought. I'm big enough to take it, but they aren't.

Neither reading nor a late movie worked to help her to sleep tonight, and she got only a few hours before dawn, which was raw and foggy and no help at all. She'd never taken anything, but she would be forced to it now; she had to have sleep so she could hold together. What would she tell the doctor? Then she realized he wouldn't need explanations; he was the Price family doctor and he'd know by now. Fletch had already been to him for stomach pains; he'd been having nervous indigestion ever since it happened. Cam claimed that Fletch was only hurting himself by trying to pray his rage out of his system instead of swearing and slamming, as *he* did.

She'd have gone somewhere in the car today if she hadn't been too groggy to trust herself behind the wheel. She kindled a small fire in the range for company and coziness, read to the children, rolled out cookies and let them have some dough to play with, all the time looking forward to their naptime when she would surely be so exhausted she could get an hour's sleep. The desire for sleep stifled everything else this morning, and that in itself was a relief.

The telephone rang when she was putting wood on the fire, and Peter scrambled up on the kitchen stool to answer it, saying, "Maybe it's Daddy! Hello!" he called brightly. Disappointment clouded him. "It's a lady, Mama."

She took the telephone from him and spoke. The responding voice was familiar and yet not, as if the speaker had slight laryngitis. "Hello, you f---ing whore, how do you like it?"

She hung up. The surprising thing was her lack of surprise. "Someone dialed a wrong number," she said to Peter.

"The lady said, 'Hello, Peter.' I thought first it was Dorri."

"That's just one of those queer things that happens with the telephone sometimes." It rang again before she'd crossed the room. Peter started for it, but she got there first. "You bitch, don't you know when a man's through with you?" It wasn't the first voice. She hung up on it.

"Communiqués from the local coven," she said to Peter, who looked perplexed for an instant and then went back to the table, where Chris was serenely rolling out his cookie dough into thin tatters. She took the telephone off the hook, laid it on the washer below it, and covered it with a cushion from the living room.

She could forbid Peter to answer, only that would be hard when he was sure each time that it was Gray calling. She thought, I could strangle her with a telephone cord and it would be entirely fitting. And then I'd brain Gray with something because a man so stupid doesn't deserve to live. She went into the bathroom and threw up her coffee.

# Chapter
# 8

She did get a nap when the boys took theirs, woke before they did, and went downstairs in time to see Kevin driving in. "Oh damn," she whispered. He was part of the whole ugly scene; yet there was something about him that forced her to smile and tell him to come in.

"I tried to call first," he said accusingly. "I kept getting the busy signal. After a while I thought something was wrong." He looked past her to where the telephone should be, and his eyes widened slightly, following the cord down to the smothering pillow.

"Oh, I took it off the hook so I could get a nap," she said casually, replacing it. "I'm just going to have a good strong cup of tea to wake me. What'll you have?"

"I'll have tea with you, I guess. Thanks." He ducked out again and brought in what he'd left on the porch, a cardboard carton with rockweed spilling over the top. Sternly he unveiled three live lobsters. "I was just down at the harbor, and I thought maybe you'd like these."

"Oh, Kevin, thank you!" she exclaimed with a good imitation of enthusiasm. "What a nice surprise! The boys and I will feast tonight. Look, put them back out where it's cool and I'll tend to them after we have our tea."

Kevin's smile cracked his severity. He was so pleased whenever she showed the right reaction, as if bit by bit he were erasing his complicity in the crime.

The telephone rang. She stood, teakettle in hand, staring at it as if it were Dorri herself spewing malevolence. "Would you answer that?" she asked Kevin.

"Sure." He reached out a long arm. "Hello!" She could dimly hear the voice at the other end; she saw Kevin's puzzlement and then his change of color. Suddenly he burst into a musical and incomprehensible speech that seemed to go on and on. The caller hung up with an emphasis audible to Astrid. Kevin gave Astrid a pleased and cocky grin.

Shaken as she was, Astrid had to laugh. "Kevin, what in heck was all that? What did you *say?*"

"Oh, that was all my Finnish strung together. Swear words, clean words, names of things—anything I could think of. One of my grandmothers is Finnish." The grin disappeared. "That was Mavis Carter. She's got a funny little stutter she can't hide."

"Dorri disguised her voice with me, but Peter recognized it. They were calling in schooltime this morning, and I can't understand that."

"Oh, Dorri's either left or been kicked out. She just showed up there that one day to tell her glad tidings, and she's never been back. Mavis has been in and out so much she's flunking the whole year."

"So they're alone in that apartment while Gray's at work on the wing," she said thoughtfully.

"Say the word and I'll go over there and ram their dirt down their throats." He doubled a big fist.

"And you'd be arrested for assault and probably rape. No, Kevin. I'll think of something." The telephone rang again and this time she answered it. Dorri's distorted voice suggested what she could do with herself.

"Do you spell that with an *f* or with *ph?*" Astrid asked pedantically. "And does it end in *k* or do you use the *q-u-e* ending?"

In frustration Dorri yelled the word four times at her and slammed down the telephone.

"Well, we can't keep this up," said Astrid, "even with a wandering Finn to answer. I guess I'll have to talk to him about it."

"She'll swear she never did it; it was somebody else trying to get her into trouble. And the tears could drown an elephant. She's pulled it on me, Astrid."

The telephone rang again. This time Kevin made a long tigerish spring at it, smiling ferociously, and became a Finn again. Then he halted and said flatly, "Who is this, please? Oh, hi, Dinah. No, she's right here."

"Who's Kevin hiding from behind that lingo?" Dinah asked in amusement. "Legions of women?"

"I don't know, but he's been entertaining us with it."

"He's a good kid. Listen, I just wanted to know from your own lips that you haven't given in yet, even if Carrie's telling how they went all the way to Portland to get the diamond and specially engraved wedding rings."

Astrid leaned against the wall and shut her eyes.

"Are you all right?" Dinah called to her.

"Yes. No, I haven't given in."

"Oh, great." Dinah sighed. "I just wanted to be able to refute or deny or whatever."

"Do me a favor and don't say anything. Pretend you don't know anything or don't care. You do a good job of looking enigmatic."

"Do I?" Dinah laughed. "Okay. I guess maybe you're right. Least said, soonest mended."

After they said goodbye, she wondered why the victim had to become everybody's victim; why suddenly her private life had to be turned inside out, with all these people lying or gossiping and watching avidly to see what happened in tomorrow's installment.

The boys were waking up. Kevin, who had been watching her with worry creasing his bony young face, said, "How about me taking them for a long walk?"

"Kevin, they'd love it," she said ardently. "And so would I."

"I thought you would," he said with satisfaction. "You can sit down and put your feet up and have your tea."

"You never had yours—"

"That's okay."

He helped get the boys into their boots and jackets, and she gave them each a couple of cookies to start out with. She watched from the porch as they set up the drive and soon disappeared in the fog and among the spruces. She put water on for the lobsters, then made her tea and put her feet up as Kevin had ordered. For the boys he was a grown-up male presence and helped to keep them from missing their father every minute of the day. Considering his part in the conspiracy, it was ironic. And how long would it help? If their dreams and the crying spells and the restless sleep happened more and more, what then?

Cam's pick-up shot down the drive. The workday was still going on, so the sight of him gave her a scare; but when she went out to meet him, he yelled "Don't worry!" as he got out. "I had to make a fast trip to Williston to see if some windows have come in yet, so I thought I'd drop around on the way back and see how you were. I saw Kevin and the boys up the road talking over the wall to the Lowells' ponies."

"I'm all right, same as I was the last time you asked."

"Hell, I guess I just didn't want to get back to the job. I came out of that shop so damned mad I could spit nails, and it's no sense telling Fletch. No sense telling you either, dammit."

"I've been trying to have a cup of tea. Come in and have one with me, if you're in no hurry, and tell me what you're mad about."

"You really want to know?" He followed her in. "Where'd you get the lobsters?"

"Kevin brought them."

"Nice kid. Here, I'll put them in the kettle." Masterfully he took over and she allowed him to, though she was perfectly capable. "Well, I was standing around over there passing the time of day with some of the guys when a man came in and started twitting me about Gray breaking loose and chasing after some choice young stuff. Heard his wife had caught him with the sitter and thrown him out, and now they're shacked up together and getting married as soon as the divorce comes through. I didn't know whether to knock his dentures down his gullet or rip them out and jump on them."

She poured his tea with a perfectly steady hand, her face set, and he said angrily, "You didn't really want to hear that, did you? But what I want to know is, are you going through with the divorce?'"

"No. What did you do to the man?"

"I just grinned and said, 'Sounds like a soap opera, doesn't it?' Threw him a mite off balance. But my God, Astrid, that damfool brother of mine needs his head taken off and put on right."

"Between Dorri and Carrie, it will be done. Give them time."

"And Fletch walks the road nights because he can't sleep and prays for Gray's soul. I'm not knocking Fletch. There's nobody I respect more. He's a true believer, and he tries to live up to what he believes. But this has punched him in the gut so hard I think half the time he's praying for the strength to control himself."

"I hope he doesn't hear this latest garbage." She lifted her cup and had to put it down again because her hands were shaking.

He saw and was disturbed. "Aw, Astrid, I shouldn't have told you."

"I'd already heard it, Cam, and more." Back in her mind the calls still persisted, living fragments of nightmare. *Don't you know when a man's through with you?* "Besides, you're such a great cusser. It's like a good strong gale of wind blowing through here."

He laughed. "And you're a great sport. I don't know how you do it. Hey, you'd better set your timer for those lobsters." She did so, and they sat having tea and new cookies in outward serenity, talking gardens and the possibility of a late frost.

When he left she walked out to the truck with him. He said diffidently, "I don't want to put any ideas in your head to make you worry, but Harriet was wondering if you're nervous at night here, with these kids racing around."

"Knock on wood." She rapped on the porch railing. "They've never been down to this end of town yet, maybe because there's only one road in and out of it. And we have such a good constable on call down here too. The ones who used to threaten Gray so long ago never took a chance on coming here for all they said over the telephone."

"Hell, they're all grown up and gone respectable—mostly—now. But nowadays these kids don't fear God, man, or the devil. They just like to raise hell. A bunch of them drove by a summer place on Amity Point last night, throwing stuff at the house, broke some windows, and they had their plates covered as well as wearing ski masks. That's the latest, the little bastards."

"Well, if I hear or see anything I don't like, I'll call George, and he and the sheriff's patrol can meet them right up there on the black road on their way out of here."

"That's right," Cam said, "there's no chance for a quick getaway here. Unless they come by boat," he added dubiously.

"Thanks, Cam," she said. "You're making me feel *so* secure. I never worried before, but now I think I'd better dig Gray's revolver out and do some target practice."

"Oh, God, don't do that!" he exclaimed. "Leave it where it is, or hide it even deeper! You could get shot, or one of the kids, or some Cade will be having you in court for assault with a dangerous weapon!"

"I'd shoot him outside the house, then drag him over the sill and say I shot him *inside*, in self-defense." She laughed at his expression. "Cam, I don't even know where it is! We used to do some target shooting, but when Peter started walking, Gray got nervous and put it away. He must have told me where, but I don't remember."

"Then leave it decently buried," said Cam fervently. He gave her a rough brotherly hug and got into the truck. She was glad no call had been made while he was there; she could imagine him charging back up the road, across the Williston bridge and down the other side to Partridge Point, and rubbing yellow soap over Dorri's teeth. She deserved it, but Cam and the rest of the family would pay for it in some form or another.

The boys came back in a good mood, smelling of ponies and lambs because they'd been given a tour of the Lowell farm. "I can't thank you enough, Kevin," Astrid told him.

"Look, about those calls—"

"She won't call tonight because he'll be there."

"Yes, but what about tomorrow? I'm trying to think of something, Astrid. I'll let you know." He was appealingly bright-eyed and anxious. So Dorri was sensitive, but Kevin would just get over everything, as if it were chicken pox. What a lot of—she startled herself and changed the word she'd almost said to *bilge*.

Peter had a crying spell before he went to bed that night, and Chris cried because Peter did. She held them both in the rocking chair, sang and rocked, sang and rocked, while her voice grew croakier and croakier. It gave great realism to "The Frog and the Crow," she thought. When the children became so heavy that she was aching, she had to rouse them to get them upstairs, and then there was another session to settle them down. They had always gone so agreeably to bed, and slept so well, that this was frightening, and in her own exhaustion she was afraid that they were being permanently scarred.

As Gray had been a good husband to her, always there when she was frightened or worried, he had been a good father, happy when the children were born, not afraid to bathe and change the newborns, firm and patient with toddlers, later always ready for conversation with his boys. Now he was victimizing them. It was hard to believe.

As she came downstairs she was aching with tiredness and thought of a warm shower, aspirin, bed. The telephone began to ring. "If this is Gray," she muttered, "his ear's about to be burned off. Hello!" she said savagely.

The short silence warned her, but not fast enough for her to hang up on it. Not Dorri's voice, but the other one with the slight excited stutter, probably coming through a handkerchief, chanted, "B-bitch, bitch, bitch, k-k-kiss my—"

"You have a very limited vocabulary, Mavis," Astrid said and hung up. "So Snow White has you working for her when she can't call herself," she observed. She took her shower, and if the telephone rang while she was in the bathroom, she didn't know. She came out, remembering and then severely rejecting the memory of finding Gray at the table in the dusk last night.

She went around the house locking the doors, including the one from the cellar, and all the downstairs windows. Then she drew the kitchen curtains across and put off all the lights except the reading light by the rocking chair, propped her feet on another chair, and tried to read one of the mysteries she'd bought uptown the other day.

Nothing happened except that she began to feel drowsy.

The girl must have been alone in the house when she called, but probably some of her family had come home since then. There'd be no more disturbance tonight. Now, if only she could get to bed without losing this precious drowsiness.

She was halfway up the front stairs when the telephone rang again, so startling in the hush it seemed vicious of itself, determined to break up Peter's fragile sleep. She nearly fell down the stairs in her hurry, cracked her elbow on the door casing, fumbled for the phone in the dark and almost dropped it, all the time praying, "Let it be *somebody!*" Meaning Nora or Dinah.

There was a soft chuckle. "G-gotcha that t-time. Too bad you didn't br-break your f---ing neck. Then he'd b-b-be rid of you."

"My, you certainly have a way with words, Mavis," Astrid said. "I'll talk to your parents tomorrow." The telephone slammed down so hard it hurt Astrid's ears. She took her own telephone off the hook and buried it under sofa cushions again on top of the washer.

She was wide awake now, but with the wonderful, lucid tranquility of supreme rage. She was safe in the eye of the hurricane. "Something has got to be done," she announced aloud. "Something *will* be done." Feeling like this, she could accomplish anything.

# Chapter
# 9

Exhilaration faded toward futility, loss of hope, an exhaustion that was worse than before. She had never been a pill-taker, but as the hours moved dismally on she wished for a tranquilizer. Still, if she went to bottom (what a wonderful thought! Hours and hours of not knowing!), what about the children? She had visions of flash fires, bone-breaking falls down the back stairs, sudden attacks of sickness. At the very least they could have nightmares and call out to be saved, and what if she didn't hear?

No, tranquilizers were out. But it was time to accept an offer of help from either Nora or Harriet. If one of them would take the boys for a day, she could get some sleep then. She got up feeling beaten down physically as well as mentally. Her mouth tasted bad and her eyes felt full of splinters. She thought with dull humor, A dirty phone call right now wouldn't raise one hackle on me.

She made some tea and squeezed in a good amount of lemon juice and drank it as hot as she could. Then she still sat at the table and rested her head in her hands, closed her eyes, and slipped dizzily into a half doze.

She dreamed that a giant woodpecker was trying to demolish the house. Reluctantly dragged awake, she knew someone was tapping, very softly, at the back door. The sunrise was filling the room. She looked out a back window, but the dooryard was empty except for birds. The tapping still went on, and someone was saying her name through the door in a loud whisper.

"Who is it?" she asked.

"Kevin."

She opened the door. He was nervous and apologetic, acting as if he were trying not to see her in her robe, though it was modest and made for warmth rather than charm. "I didn't want to wake up the kids," he went on in his hoarse whisper, "so I left my car up the lane. Nobody can see it from the road, either. I got up early to bring you this before school." He was carrying a small case. "Astrid, are you okay? You look kind of sick. Should I get somebody?"

"It's lack of sleep, that's all. I had a couple of calls last night from Rebecca of Sunnybrook Farm. Do you know that in Scotland a mavis is a songbird? Some singer, our Mavis."

"No kidding!" He was aghast. "You mean Dorri's got her working around the clock for her?"

"Well, until about ten last night anyway. That reminds me." She exhumed the telephone and hung it up. Moving fast made her feel squeamish. "What's the tape recorder for?"

"Listen, I worked this all out last night. I practiced with the extension in my folks' room. I didn't tell 'em why, I just said it was an experiment. Heck, I couldn't keep it a secret, with the younger kids around. Now, this is all you have to do."

She sat down and tried to follow.

"Here's a couple of calls I made to another guy. You can see how clear they came through." He played the tape for her. She heard him shushing the younger children, who wanted to be recorded too, and then there was the whir of the dial, the answer at the other end, and a conversation about baseball practice and the graduation exercises. There were both music and voices in the background.

"That was in *his* house," Kevin said. "Whenever he spoke I held the mike right to the telephone, see?" He was luminous with pride. "So, whenever you answer, press these two keys and that will start recording. If it's just an ordinary call you can turn it off again by this key. Here's the directions, in case you forget." He gave her a booklet.

"My head's going around now, trying to concentrate with no sleep," she admitted. "But that's like a machine my parents used in their teaching, and I taped things on it sometimes, so I guess I'll manage all right."

"You notice how little distortion there was. The sound's about as true as you can get with a machine like this."

"Yes, your voice sounded very natural. I'll do my best, Kevin. I'll have to, after all the trouble you've gone to." You see? she said to herself. I can't even give in and stay defeated. I've gone and nailed myself to the mast.

"I'm the one who has to do an awful lot," he said gruffly. "I think sometimes I'll never be able to make it up."

"Kevin, you didn't cause this thing. You knew about it, but you didn't *do* it, and you certainly didn't know it would go this far."

"But where was my *brain?*" he asked despairingly. "I must've been out of my skull! It was wrong in the first place, whatever it was! And I knew it, but it didn't seem to matter. It was like being stoned all the time. Well, I'd better get going." He almost groped for the door, muttering, "Red and I are supposed to be pitching a few balls before school this morning. That's what I told my mother when I left early."

"Well, I appreciate this, Kevin," she said. If she shut her eyes the room rocked.

"I'll check around tonight and see what happened." He got the door open finally, but still didn't give her a direct look.

"All right. Maybe she won't dare try it again, though. I think I scared Mavis last night."

"Dorri doesn't scare. She thinks she can talk her way out of everything. But if we get her on tape, she'll have a hell of a hard time. Excuse me, Astrid. . . . So long."

He took off, almost running.

She set the tape recorder on the washer under the telephone, with magazines piled in front so Peter wouldn't notice it. Then she called Nora, who was delighted to be of use. She was going to the post office to mail a package and she would drive from there to get the boys; she wouldn't stop, because the plumber was coming. "I'll keep them all day, dear. We'll have a wonderful time, and you get a good sleep."

Knowing they were going to Uncle Fletch's, to play with their cousins' outgrown toys, got the boys through the period when they woke up asking for Gray and then turned bad-tempered or, what was worse, silent.

Once she saw them off with Nora, all three talking

cheerfully, and she had a whole day to herself, she felt lightheaded with relief as well as fatigue and even wondered if it would be possible to arrange a visit with Gray; they could tell the boys he'd come home from the distant job just to see them. An afternoon with the boys might be exactly the thing to start him thinking in another direction, away from Dorri.

After all, he was a grown man and she was still a kid, for all he praised her sensitivity and maturity. By now he must have faced some realities; if not, there were the phone calls. Astrid had hoped for no more of them, but now she wanted some evidence that would cauterize and seal off his infatuation.

She took the tape recorder upstairs with her and put it by the telephone on the stand beside her and Gray's bed. She hadn't slept in there since he left, but today just to lie down anywhere was good. She covered up with a spare blanket and lay listening to the swallows and a distant conclave of crows who might have discovered an owl. Boats came and went in the cove. She began to float. *Heaven . . .*

The telephone rang and the sound ran her through like a sword. She fumbled but knew enough to press the right buttons. Gray must have just gone to work, she thought.

It was Dorri all right. "I don't know why you bother to try to change your voice, Dorri," Astrid said, sounding bored.

"Why don't you give him up, you old cow? He can't even stand the sight of you. He'd never have married you, but you tricked him. He told me."

She didn't believe it, but her stomach roiled anyway. "Then you tell *me* about it, Dorri," she said. Dorri had added more words to her working vocabulary today. She used them now and hung up in a temper.

Astrid turned off the tape recorder and fell back against the pillows. The sense of utter disbelief that had been with her from the first had not grown any less with time. Now she felt as much disgust as if she'd found bedbugs crawling among her sheets. It was enough to make her want to end everything here and now, take the boys and go somewhere far away, never speak to Gray again, and tell the children he was dead.

But she would not. This was their home; Gray had bought it from her parents. Gray was still theirs too. He would get over this, he *had* to; all you had to do was hang on. Sometimes hanging on was hell, but if you could, maybe you'd come through almost in one piece. Couples had weathered worse things, though at this moment she couldn't think of anything worse.

Oh, yes, you can, she thought sardonically. What if you found out Gray was in love with a boy? What if he had a sex-change operation and suddenly became the boys' aunt? Just be thankful you don't have to explain *that* to them.

She broke into gasps of laughter and ended up by crying as hard as the boys did. Afterward she felt calm, almost rested. When the telephone rang again, she was ready, but it was Dinah this time, who asked her to bring the boys to a cook-out the next night. She apologized for calling when Astrid told her she was trying to get some sleep.

"You'd better entomb the phone in a bureau drawer under a lot of sweaters."

"I'm going to. But we'd love the cook-out, Dine. Thanks."

The third call was Dorri again. This time she pitched

into Astrid with a long speech, ordering her to stop being a bitch in the manger, holding onto a man whom she was incapable of pleasing anyway because she was frigid; and Peter wasn't *his*, but she'd made him think so because he was so goodhearted. And if she didn't get the divorce, Dorri and Gray knew how to manage it, so he'd get the divorce and the kids too.

It was punctuated at intervals with the nouns and adjectives which were now losing their shock value through overuse. "That'll do, Dorri," Astrid said at last, briskly. "I'll have a word with the telephone company tomorrow."

"Who'd believe a jealous wife?" Dorri jeered.

"Well, we can find out, can't we?" She hung up, turned off the tape recorder, and interred the telephone in the blanket chest. Then she slept.

Nora and Fletch returned the boys after an early supper. With seven hours of solid sleep behind her, she looked and acted well, and she knew they were reassured.

Fletch was thinner than he'd been a week ago and had new lines in his face. He was quiet, not with his usual peaceful aura, but with an obviously painful preoccupation. She knew he wasn't worried only about her, but about Gray himself; to Fletch a man's soul was an immortal gift, beyond price, and for his brother to endanger his soul would be a real horror for Fletch. And, being the man he was, Fletch was probably concerned for Dorri's soul too.

The boys were ready for baths and bed. They had enough to tell her so that she was spared singing songs, reading stories, and answering questions about Daddy. She let them talk themselves out. In the morning she would tell them about the cook-out. There must be something every morning to get them all past that terrible moment of waking without Gray.

Kevin came while she was eating her light supper, and they took the machine into the living room and played back the tape. It was so good that Kevin let out a wild whoop, which he quickly stifled. Over his hand his eyes sparkled with triumph.

"I wish I could call Gray to make a date," Astrid said. "But I don't know who owns the place over there. Do you?" He shook his head. "Would you feel cheated if I asked you to stay with the kids and I went over there without you?"

"I don't want to go!" he said violently. "I don't want to see them together!"

"Then I'll go right now and take a chance on catching them in. If I can't, I'll go around tomorrow while he's working."

"Don't let her get her hands on that tape recorder."

"Don't worry. Get yourself something to eat, Kevin. The television won't bother the boys if you don't run it full blast."

He went out to the car with her, saying anxiously, "And don't let her make a grab for that tape, either. I don't know if you should go alone."

"I won't talk to her without Gray, Kevin. Now you've done your part and I'll do mine." She smiled and gave him a pat on the shoulder. He stood watching her drive out.

Her long rest and the solid evidence on the seat beside her made her feel more strong and confident than she'd felt at any time since Gray had left. She wore a blue dress and a matching Fair Isle cardigan that Gray had always liked; she had some color under her new tan, and her hair was freshly washed. Dorri would see no haggard, frantic woman. Bitch in the manger. "Frigid *indeed!*" she said with vigorous contempt. And the rotten bit about Peter— wait until Gray heard that, along with all the other stuff he was supposed to have told.

She drove through Williston and down the other side of the river. In the sunset light it was a broad, rose-tinted stream flowing between green meadows and patches of rich dark fir forest and bright-leaved hardwoods. The wild shadbushes shimmered everything like young girls in filmy white, a pretty image suddenly turned ugly for her; Dorri looking angelic in bridal white, exchanging those engraved wedding bands with Gray.

The band on her own finger seemed to burn to the bone; everything about her looked unfamiliar and she was going too fast. She eased up her foot, coasted to the side of the road, and sat there trying to pull herself together. She had that now familiar sensation that her brain was about to explode.

After this crisis she had good control again and kept her mind on her driving. She knew where Partridge Point was; she turned off at the Wells Corner Church and followed a narrow, hard-packed gravel road between stone walls and arching maples.

The big white house faced down the river toward the open sea, and the three-car garage wing was nearest the road, but the wide windows of its upstairs apartment must have also had a good view. Part of the new wing on the other side was visible to Astrid just before she turned onto the blacktop parking area outside the garage doors and stopped beside Gray's pick-up. When she turned off the ignition the mild twilight was instantly loud, not with peepers and late birdcalls but rock music from the open windows above. That was to her an advantage; no one had heard or seen her arrive.

She went up the outside staircase to the balcony, carrying the tape recorder. She knocked firmly on the door. A light came on inside and Dorri yelled above the racket, "I'll get it, Doll!" Astrid winced at that.

Dorri opened the door and the look of consternation on her face was worth a good deal. "Your mouth is open," said Astrid and walked in past her. "Is Gray here?"

"Hey!" Dorri tried to get in front of her. "You can't come barging in here like that!"

"Can't I?" She kept on advancing, and after a moment Dorri moved aside. She was very red and shrill.

"Who do you think you are?"

"I don't *think*, I know who I am. Gray's wife. Gray, are you here?" she called, looking around the big room. He came in from another room, bare-legged, tying a short, bright robe around him. His hair was wet. His consternation was different from Dorri's; it gave her no triumph but a needle of pain in the midriff. He must feel like a fool in that thing, she thought. He looked speechlessly at her and she smiled.

"Hello, Doll. I never thought of you as a doll before. Funny, I always saw you as a man. Are you two playing Ken and Barbie Doll?"

"Gray!" Dorri yelped. "Get her out of here!" She rushed to him and he put an arm around her, without taking his eyes off Astrid. He seemed more wary and embarrassed than hostile. Dorri wrapped both arms around him and flattened herself against him. To show me, Astrid thought. Light flashed off the diamond. Again she felt the pure exhilaration of great rage. In a mood like this you would kill or be killed without feeling it.

"What do you want, Astrid?" Gray asked. "Are the children all right?"

"If they weren't, I'd have asked the police to locate you," she said. "A cruiser turning in here would give you quite a turn, wouldn't it? You'd think somebody'd sworn out a complaint at last.... Well, that can happen yet, though it might not be the one you're expecting."

She set the case on the coffee table.

"What's *that?*" Dorri demanded tearfully, wrapping herself even tighter around Gray.

"You can see it's a tape recorder, not a bomb," said Astrid reasonably. "Now, Gray, if I can have your attention, please."

She pressed the PLAY button. The sound started in the middle of one peal of the telephone. Dorri guessed and exclaimed too soon, "What's that got to do with *us?*"

"For God's sake," Gray said, "what's this for, Astrid?"

"Wait for the goody, love," she said.

She was heard saying, "Hello." Then Dorri took over, husky, drawling, arrogant, and filthy. Astrid watched the two, Gray paling, his arm dropping away from the girl, who clung even harder. She turned a dead white, her eyes staring so that she did look like a doll. When the two calls had been played through, Astrid shut off the machine.

"You can see how Dorri's been enriching her vocabulary," she explained. "She shows great promise, don't you think? I can play it again."

"You don't have to," said Gray.

"These are just from today. I didn't record yesterday's and last night's."

"Last night?" He grabbed on that. "But I was here."

"Mavis had the night patrol from her home or wherever she hangs out when she's not here. During the day they took turns from here. They'll be on the bill, Gray, because they're toll calls."

"It's a put-up job, Gray!" Dorri cried. The diamond sparkled as she grabbed his shoulders and tried to turn him toward her. "She's got somebody to imitate me—she'd do *anything*. She hates me because I've got you—"

"She's not a liar," said Gray. He finally took her by the arms and put her away from him, not roughly, but she threw herself violently backward onto the sofa as if she'd been pushed and began to cry.

Now you know that she's just a nasty little kid, Gray, Astrid thought, keeping her face disciplined. She didn't feel like smiling; listening to the tape had brought back all the reaction the original calls had produced. "I expect you to put a stop to this. I had to have proof so you'd know."

He seemed dazed. Dorri's weeping grew in volume. Enough tears to drown an elephant, Kevin had said. Well, she was off to a good start.

"Gray, Gray!" Dorri moaned. She sprang up and rushed blindly at him. "She won't let you go! She knows you love me but she can't stand it. I was just trying to *make* her—maybe it was wrong, but it's only because I love you so! Gray, everybody hates me because of you—you're all I've got—you can't turn against me! I'll kill myself!" she shrieked and ran into the bathroom and slammed and locked the door.

"Dorri!" Gray yelled at her and grabbed the doorknob and shook it. On the other side she wailed incoherently, and glass broke. "*Dorri!*"

"I'm going to slash my wrists," she babbled between choking sobs. "I'll really do it this time! You hate me, and it's all her fault!"

"I don't hate you!"

"You're going to walk out on me!"

"No, I'm not!"

Pathetic gaspings and snufflings. Then weakly: "Promise?"

"Yes, I promise. Now open the door."

"I'll take this tape to the telephone company if there are any more calls," Astrid said to his back and walked out before Dorri could emerge in triumph from the bathroom and throw herself into Gray's arms.

"That futile, besotted idiot!" she raged as she drove away. *I'll really do it this time.* Was that how she got him that night?

Kevin had been right. They probably stopped the calls, but they hadn't stopped anything else. She averted her conscious mind from the prospect of those two spending half the night in an orgy of repentance and forgiveness, because she had to keep it on her driving if her children weren't to lose mother as well as father.

**K**evin said gloomily, "Maybe if you'd kept him talking while she was crashing around in there, she'd have really done it just to show him."

"Yes, and what a mess for everybody, and I don't mean the blood! Whatever happened would get into the papers. And if she died, I'd be an accessory. I don't want her dead, Kevin, but just out of our lives."

Kevin looked even more depressed.

"Cheer up, you've helped me put a stop to the calls," she told him, "and he may start thinking a little more clearly when he remembers later on all that he heard on those tapes. I'm not going to let this get me down, and don't you go around worrying either. Your graduation's coming soon, and this should be a good happy time for you."

He nodded without conviction. "Oh, I made a note of your calls. Harriet was one, and George Rollins wants to know right off if anyone comes around here at night and makes you nervous. Somebody called him yesterday about an outboard cruising in and out of Harper's Cove. Unregistered. Anyway, he says call him. Even if it turns out to be a false alarm he'd rather check up on it than not."

"Sounds as if everybody knows by now that I'm alone."

"How could they help it? If Gray wanted to keep it quiet, Carrie and Dorri have got a news network all their own. Hey!" He stared at her, mouth open. "I just remembered! Dorri dated one of those Cade kids once. Damon. I thought she left him for *me*." His grin was sour. "I thought she'd raised her standards and was going in for class instead of the local Mafia. Now I know where I fitted in."

"No wonder Carrie's so eager to make the best of things," said Astrid.

"Yeah, there was some scuttlebutt about her almost getting caught with them when they were raising hell one night. The sheriff's patrol was looking for them, and they managed to drop her in a woodroad somewhere, and she had to walk home alone, after midnight. After that she cooled it. But, Astrid," he said anxiously, "if she's still friendly with him, she might get him to give you a hard time. And if nobody caught him, you couldn't prove she had anything to do with it."

"What is this power she has over men to make them do what she wants?" Astrid inquired, and Kevin turned scarlet.

After he left, she considered returning her calls, but she thought she was too keyed up by the evening to make sense. She had a long hot bath and made a mug of cocoa to sip while she read in bed.

The children slept well all night. It was as if Kevin's masculine influence in the house had started them off right. She slept fairly well herself and woke up in a slightly optimistic mood. At least Gray had some hard facts to mull over while he worked today, unless Dorri was so fabulously talented in bed that nothing else she might do, short of moonlighting as a prostitute, could influence him against her.

With her first cup of coffee, Astrid planned an outdoor day for the boys; they could start painting the dory, and they'd have the cook-out to look forward to. She told them about both things when they woke up, so they began breakfast in a happy frame of mind, and while they were eating she returned Harriet's call. It was an invitation to Sunday dinner, and she accepted. Then she called George Rollins, the constable for this end of town, and thanked him for his concern.

"Is there really anything to worry about, George?" she asked him.

"I wouldn't lose any sleep about it," he said. "But just sleep handy to a telephone. The sheriff's department and the State Police and the local law-enforcement officers in three towns are all working together to get these kids out of everybody's hair, so if any strange boat comes into your cove at night, or any strange car comes down your road, you *call*. Keep your car in the barn, locked, and all the barn doors locked too so nobody can steal your battery, and if you have anything worth swiping in the fishhouse, keep that locked too."

"What was so special about that outboard in Harper's Cove?"

"Two people wearing ski masks in a warm May evening."

"That gives me the horrors," she said. "Not that I'm *afraid* of them. I know they don't go in for murder and so forth, just general hell-raising and thievery. But it's the whole idea of their ranging far and wide so you can't feel that anything's safe any more. It used to be only in the cities that you had to keep everything locked up tight."

"Yeah, well, we're getting more civilized up here all the time," he said dryly. "They call it progress."

After breakfast, she and the boys went down to the shore to look over the paint supplies in the fishhouse. "We'll paint her all the colors of the rainbow if we have to," she told them.

"Oh boy!" Peter was radiant. "That'll be pretty!"

"Oh boy!" Chris echoed. She glanced around at the contents of the building. She couldn't imagine anyone easily getting the skiff down from the loft, or wanting the clam hoes and spare oars and the rest of the clutch, useful or otherwise, that collected in a fishhouse. But there was also a well-equipped workbench, and tools were an important item in the world of theft. She found a couple of padlocks and their keys in one of the bench drawers. It was going to be a nuisance to have to think of locks all the time, but it was nothing at all when she considered her chief preoccupation these days.

They settled on bright blue for the dory. Chris daubed happily away at the stern. Peter was more skillful at the bow, holding his tongue just right, carefully drawing the brush out. "Daddy'll be some surprised when he comes home," he said contentedly.

"He sure will be."

"Then we can all go out for a row. Maybe *I* can row us." The old outboard motor had given up last fall, and they were to have bought a new one this summer.

"While we're waiting, we'll get somebody to bring the

skiff down, Peter, after we finish the dory, and you can start learning to row her, because she's smaller. In the meantime you can be thinking of a good name."

"I know it already! *Ibex.* I is for Ibex. That's my most favorite word."

"One of mine too," said Astrid.

When they went back to the house for lunch, she had cleaned the paint off their hands with kerosene on a rag, and now she stood them on chairs at the kitchen sink, filled a basin with warm water, and gave them each a cake of soap. But Chris was enchanted with the scent of kerosene and didn't want to lose it. He kept sniffing at his fingers.

"It's dewicious!" he exclaimed, at which Peter went into great bursts of overdone laughter. "Dewicious, dewicious! Everybody knows it's *delushious,* you dope!"

Chris's lower lip rolled out, trembling.

"Everybody knows it's *delicious,*" she corrected Peter. "And nobody's a dope around here. We're all sparkling and brilliant."

"Daddy too," he said fiercely.

"Daddy's the most sparkling and brilliant of us all. Let's eat this *delicious* lunch."

While the boys slept, Astrid lay in a deck chair out front and tried to nap. It didn't work, and she was thinking of going back into the house and looking for some poetry when Carrie Sears came around the corner. Astrid hadn't heard the car come in; surprised and annoyed, she could simply stare at Carrie for a moment.

But Carrie, though solemn, seemed pleased with herself. "I *thought* the babies would be having their naps."

"They'll be waking up any time now," Astrid warned her.

"I'll only be a minute. I just came from across the river. Well, I took the children a salmon casserole; it's Dorri's favorite."

So Gray was a child now, was he? Just one of the kids? Carrie's expression changed from smug to flustered, and Astrid wondered what her own was, to produce this effect.

"Now, Astrid," Carrie said in a rush, "I don't *condone* these actions, and I've told Dorri I'd never step over her doorstep until she was married, but when she called up this morning she was in such a *state*. Well, I'm her mother after all, and right now she's a mighty scared little girl." She grew red-faced and talked even faster. "So I took the casserole over—she's no cook—and she threw herself into my arms and told me how sorry she was, but things just had to be this way, because she and—"

A stop, a cleared throat, and a shift of emotional gears. "Maybe they do love each other," she said austerely, "but I told her that was no excuse for tormenting you over the telephone. No excuse at *all*."

"Oh, she told you about it?" Astrid sounded mildly curious. "And did she tell you about the language she used and having Mavis call me at night?"

"She felt just awful. So ashamed! And she wanted to tell me herself before you—before anyone else did. She said she was just so upset because you won't start the divorce, she didn't know what she was doing. And that's the way she's always been, Astrid," Carrie said earnestly. "She gets her heart set on anything, she goes all to pieces when she doesn't get it. When she was a tiny thing she used to hold her breath until she turned blue and even pass out. Well, she only did that once or twice before Rupe and I realized what a high-strung young one we had."

Astrid couldn't think of anything to say, so she didn't speak and her silence made Carrie even more frantically voluble. "You know how young girls are; you were one not so long ago. She's been planning a September wedding; she's designing her gown and one for her maid of honor—"

"Her maid of *what?*" said Astrid.

Even Carrie couldn't miss that. Her face blotched deeply under the flush. "Well, what about *him?*" she demanded stridently. "It's just our decency and consideration for his family and for you and your children that keeps us from having him thrown into jail!"

"Are you sure it's that, Carrie?" she asked softly. "Isn't it the fact that she's off your hands? Or will be, if I'd just cooperate?"

"I don't know who's running around gossiping," said Carrie with an attempt at dignity, "but I will admit that she's always been attracted to wild boys, and I was always afraid she'd be found dead in a ditch somewhere. It was a real relief when she took up with Kevin Whitehouse. Then it turned out that—well, at least Gray's a grown man, and nobody could ever call him wild."

"Maybe not wild, but a few other things."

"Listen to you, you're disgusted with him!" Carrie exclaimed. "How can you want to hold on to him, then? I'd be too proud to hang on to a man that's treated me the way he's treated you!"

"Maybe I'm not proud," said Astrid reasonably. "I wouldn't think of divorcing him for this any more than I would if he had a broken leg or pneumonia."

"Don't talk so foolish." Carrie's eyes filled with tears. "Look, maybe we can talk her out of a big wedding—we can't pay for anything like that, and I'm sure Gray doesn't want anything conspicuous—"

"Carrie, I don't want to be rude, but we've no more to discuss. If Dorri's decided she wants my husband, and I'm supposed to give in because nobody in her little life has ever said *no* to her and made it stick, then it's time somebody did." She walked toward the corner of the house and Carrie, as if hypnotized, walked along with her. Astrid was sorry for her, apart from her irritation and a squeamish disgust.

At the car, Carrie made another attempt. "Don't you want a new life of your own?"

"No, I loved my old life. I don't want to give it up."

"You don't know Dorri. She can twist them all around her little finger. You thought she was a wonderful kid once yourself, didn't you?" In her bleak despair she became for a moment an honest woman. "Before you knew the other side of her? . . . Well, she's been her father's little princess for years, and now she's breaking his heart."

"Why doesn't he make her come home, then? She's still under age."

"I told you! We've never been able to make her do anything she didn't want to do."

"There must have been a time once when she was smaller than you," Astrid suggested rather cruelly. "Even if she did hold her breath. She wouldn't have died, you know." Take a lesson from this, she warned herself. Don't make monsters of the boys.

Wordlessly Carrie got into the car and slammed the door. When she had gone, Astrid still had that itchy, soiled feeling again, yet her resolution was strong. I don't accept, she thought. I *won't*. They'll just have to keep on shacking up, and when the break-up comes, as it will when the excitement goes out of it for her, then she'll run off with somebody else, and he and I can talk about his coming home.

# Chapter 11

At Dinah's cook-out on the harbor rocks that night, she asked Ben for a handful of the miniature buoys he whittled out for the children to play with and for Dinah's curtain pulls. After the boys were in bed, she fastened the padlock keys to them with the nylon baitbag twine he'd given her and lettered each buoy with the location of its padlock. The buoys were hung on hooks in the row of other household and car keys on the board inside one of the cupboard doors.

In the next three days there was no communication from Gray about the phone calls, and she'd expected some attempt to apologize, even a weak one. He didn't even use the children or money as an excuse to get in touch. She was hurt by this, which she knew was illogical in view of the one great wound she had received. She hadn't believed he could let the slanders go by, but then she hadn't believed he could do any of the other things he'd done lately, either. She tried to cultivate her cynicism, which was better than self-pity.

Kevin called one morning to ask if the lawn needed

mowing. He was busy with baseball and graduation practice, but he'd find time somehow.

"I've already mowed it."

"Oh, for Pete's sake! Why'd you do that?"

"I felt like it." There was nothing more satisfyingly exhausting than a couple of hours with a power mower on a long slant of lawn.

"What about trash for the dump?" he asked accusingly.

"I've taken it. Don't groan. The boys think the dump's as good as Disneyland. They'd like to stay for hours. Someday it won't be so easy and so cheap to entertain them. . . . Kevin, are you calling from home?"

"No, I'm in the booth by the store, on my way to school."

"What does your mother think of your coming over here to do chores? I want to be sure she and your father don't object." He didn't answer, and she said urgently, "Don't they know?"

"Yup, they know," he said. "And they know *why* I do. I had to tell them finally, because they knew I was dating her. So when the you-know-what hit the fan they kind of cornered me."

"All right, Kevin. I'll take your word for it that it's all right with them."

"Then will you have something for me to do when I get this stupid stuff over with?" he pleaded.

"You can help me launch the dory. We've got her all painted. But the haul-off needs to be put out first. And I'd like to get the skiff down from the fishhouse loft."

"Great!"

Well, I've made somebody happy today, if not me, she thought.

She did a wash that morning and went outdoors to hang
it up, preferring sunshine to the dryer whenever it was
possible. The clotheslines were beyond the barn, and the
boys were out there with her, handing clothespins to her
when they weren't looking for violets in the unshorn
grass just outside the drying area. There was a southwest
sea breeze blowing through the tops of the spruces, so
they didn't hear anything approaching until the small
bright-green car flashed down the road and into the yard,
spun in a tight circle with a groaning protest of tires and
dragging crunch of gravel, and then, with the gravel flying
in a spatter that hit the barn and the back porch, the car
was off up the lane again with a triumphant blast of the
horn.

They all three stood staring at the place where it disappeared. Then Peter shouted, "Mama, that was *Dorri!*"

"Yes, it was," she agreed.

"Why didn't she stop and give us a ride?" He was in-
dignant. "Maybe she will next time, huh?"

"Maybe." Astrid was bemused. Was this the answer to
the scene the other night? The reward for being frightened
by the Wicked Witch? Gray had done so many impossible
things that a sports car for Dorri was looking more possible by the moment. She knew now what was meant by
mind-boggling. Still bemused, she went into the open barn
and fondly patted the secondhand dark-blue Oldsmobile.
They had planned to buy a brand-new station wagon at
the end of the year, paying cash for it. But when they'd
decided he should leave his brothers and go to work on
his own, she'd simply put the new car out of mind. They
might have had to fall back on their savings.

*Their savings.* She went into the house, called the bank

in Williston, and asked for the balance on the joint account. It was eight thousand dollars less than it had been when she made the last deposit, just before the blow-up. It was now a little under *five* thousand. She filled out a withdrawal slip for four thousand, with instructions to start a new savings account in her name only. The joint checking balance was also so low that she was in danger of overdrawing. She left that as it was and arranged to start a new checking account, also in her name alone. It gave her a strange, vacant sensation, as if Gray had died.

She loaded the boys into the car and went to the post office to be sure the bank envelope went out in the late mail. She could have driven to Williston the next day and transacted the business in the bank, but she was afraid of meeting that bright-green little car, of the insulting wave and horn; worse would be to see Gray driving and Dorri buckled in smugly beside him. With savage relish she imagined the car going off the road on one of those steep sharp turns (but not with Gray in it) and ending up in a smoking mass of crumpled metal in a rocky gully; or shooting down one certain hillside out of control toward the flood tide, plunging into the water, and sinking out of sight in a matter of seconds.

Don't think like that, don't think like that! she scolded herself. At least not while you're driving! *You're* the one who could end up in the ditch, and she'd still be tearing around town in a new car that you paid for by the way you managed his pay and his home.

The day had been still and hot, but by late afternoon the fog was coming in. She took in the washing, with the boys' help; sunlit blue distances and flowering fields disappeared;

the light went cold. She wanted to run away to sunshine, but there was nowhere to go.

"Tell you what," she said to the boys, "we'll have a fire in the fireplace tonight and we'll have a picnic in front of it, and we'll sing and everything."

Both children beamed, then Peter dimmed as the day had dulled with the fog. "I wish Daddy would come." Chris's dark eyes filled. "But maybe Kevin will come, Chris," Peter said kindly. "Will he, Mama?"

"Kevin's practicing marching for graduation. This will be our very own picnic." She hoped that made it sound like a super-picnic. They were enchanted with the meal spread out on a sheet before the fireplace and making believe they were in the woods. Peter got into the spirit of the thing and was pointing out bears behind the sofa and deer walking on top of the piano. They toasted marshmallows for dessert. Then, sticky hands washed first, they worked their way through *Baby's Opera*, a child on either side of Astrid at the piano. Chris began yawning first, leaning against his mother, and while she was settling him on the sofa to listen, Peter began picking out his favorite with one finger and singing the words in a sweet, strong, true voice.

> "A jolly fat frog lived in the river swim, O!
> A comely black crow lived on the river brim, O!
> 'Come on shore, come on shore,' said the crow to the
> frog, and then O!
> 'No, you'll bite me, no, you'll bite me,' said the frog to
> the crow again, O!"

She couldn't deny that he showed signs of talent. Her parents had both been professional musicians, her mother still was, and all the Prices had good ears and voices. It can be something fine for him, she thought, watching the competent little forefinger striking the right notes. It can mean a lot of pleasure and satisfaction.

Chris, already sleep, had been able to carry a tune since he was in the playpen, humming what Peter sang. Thinking about this was comforting, it was real, it bleached out the memory of the green car.

"I like the part about the sweet music," Peter said. She sat down beside him and sang with him.

> " 'O! There is sweet music on yonder green hill, O!
> And you shall be a dancer, a dancer in yellow,
> All in yellow, all in yellow,'
> Said the crow to the frog, and then, O!
> 'All in yellow, all in yellow,'
> Said the frog to the crow again, O!"

"You play now, Mama," Peter said. They went on until an enormous yawn stopped him in the middle of a line.

"Time for bed, I think," she said. She didn't want to reach the frog's plaintive questions: *But where is the sweet music on yonder green hill, O? And where are all the dancers, the dancers in yellow?*

The verse ended with a long dash and a footnote: *Here the crow swallows the frog.* One of these days Peter was going to ask her what those words said, and she wanted the time to think up a good lie. He had enough to disturb his sleep now.

The next afternoon the man from the oil company came to give the heater its routine cleaning and put in a new filter so it would be all ready for fall. When he finished, she waited on the back porch while he wrote out a slip to leave with her to show that he had been there and what he had done. The green car came down the hill again. This time they heard it long before it showed up. The walls of spruces picked up and magnified the sound of its progress, and the horn was blaring in a jazzy rhythm. Dorri jammed on the brakes when she saw the truck in her way. She made a violent reverse over the lawn and was gone again, still sounding the horn.

"Dorri, Dorri!" Peter yelled. "Wait!"

"Good God, what was that?" asked the man. "A new rocket missile the Pentagon's trying out?"

"Yes, it's called Green Death," said Astrid.

"Well, it'd be death all right if there'd been chickens or a dog out in that road when she came blasting down. Or your kids."

"What kind of a car was that, do you know?" Astrid asked him.

"Audi. Sweet little job, runs about seven thousand. Some rich summer kid showing off, huh?" He looked embarrassed. "Maybe it's a friend of yours." He nodded at Peter. "He knows her."

"We all know her, but I can't say it's a friend."

"Well, the tires'll be gone in a week, if she lives long enough to wear 'em out. That Audi is going to end up looking like an accordion in a tree or a grout pile, like one I saw over near the quarries once. I wrote down the number in case you want it."

"Thanks!" she said in pleased surprise. "She's been down here before, but I don't intend to let it happen again. This way I can let an officer take care of it."

"Who knows, you may save her life for her, even if she doesn't seem to think much of it."

When he had gone, she made the boys come inside in case Dorri was waiting up on the black road for the truck to go. She called George Rollins, who had just come in from hauling and was having a mug-up in his kitchen. She gave him the plate number but no name. After he wrote it down he asked, "Did you recognize the driver?"

"Well, it wasn't a Cade and it wasn't somebody in a ski mask."

"You hedging, Astrid?"

She hesitated, then said, "Dorri Sears."

"Yep. Well, I know where to go see about it. I'd better check with the registry first to see who owns it and if she has a license or not. That ought to make it real interesting."

"I'd say so. Thanks, George." She appreciated his tact in not mentioning Gray's name. She wondered if the confrontation would end in Dorri's locking herself in the bathroom, breaking another glass, and threatening suicide again. She hoped that Gray would be agonizingly embarrassed by the whole episode; he deserved to be, taking their money to buy something so ridiculously expensive and then letting her drive it around. He'd really flipped if he didn't realize that she could wreck the car or be involved in a serious accident for which he would be responsible.

But maybe he didn't know about it; maybe he'd had to take the truck to Limerock for something, and she'd gone off with the car as soon as he was out of sight.

On Sunday he would have been gone three weeks. It felt much longer, not only in time but in herself. On that first scarifying day, she had believed that if he came home to her that night they could go on with their life on the other side of the affair, as if it had been a disaster to be forgotten or at least overcome. But with everything that had happened since, Gray kept changing shape and color, and she kept reacting to each transformation by one of her own; she had been wounded, saddened, disgusted, cynical, malicious, vindictive. Though she knew that such responses were natural, that it was normal even to feel murderous as long as it was just in your mind, she was shaken to find them in herself. She had not only to adjust herself to an alien Gray, but to a different Astrid.

She hated to go to bed tonight. Sometimes she slept well, sometimes badly, and tonight she was embittered and lonely, thinking of six years in that bed with Gray, six years of sleeping against his back or with his arm holding her close to him. Like his Teddy bear, she thought now.

But she remembered the last time they had made love, in the week before the end of things, and it had been as good as it ever was, maybe better; they always agreed each time that it was better than the last. The full moon had filled the room, and they had joked about its effect on them. Recollection took her by the throat.

No, she couldn't go to bed tonight. She found a movie on television, one of those dated English mysteries made on location in Cornwall. It had a pleasantly drugging effect, so that during the commercials she even began dreaming a little about taking the children to England on the rest of the savings account, and to hell with the taxes. . . . Lights flashed into the living room and aroused her.

She thought at once, *Gray is coming home!* But she knew in the next second it wasn't so. Through the mists of her drowsiness she saw him suddenly as he must see himself: a prisoner all his life inside the gentlemanly Price image, so that it was not only the family firm against which he had rebelled but everything to do with the Graham Price whom everybody else saw. Even Cam, with his jokes and his dancing and his strong language, went just so far. No, Gray, the quietest and the youngest, must go all the way.

It was an illumination but not necessarily a comforting one. If he was a prisoner, what does that make the boys and me? she questioned, shivering, on her way to see if she should call George Rollins about this car. His jailers?

She was keeping a pad and pen on the windowsill for descriptions and plate numbers. She put on the outside light and saw Cam's car in the dooryard. Cam and Harriet seemed to be having an argument, she could tell by the gestures.

And we were happy, her own argument went on. Don't tell me he wasn't happy. She had a thousand pictures stored away in her memory bank, slides in full color, to prove his content, pride, pleasure, delight. They had the normal quota of disagreements, she supposed, but nothing that hadn't been talked out and mended. Or so she'd always believed.

She opened the back door, and Cam got out of the car, saying, "I *told* you she was still up."

"It's not that late," she called. "In fact, it's too early for you two to end your Friday night. Or are you just beginning it?"

"We broke it off early tonight." Cam came up the steps and kissed her cheek.

Harriet followed, sputtering, "I told him you had a hard time sleeping sometimes, and went to bed early. But you know how these Prices are."

"I'm finding out more all the time," said Astrid. "Wow,

do you two look *glamorous*. Nice to see how the other half lives." She'd always loved dancing, and Gray was a good dancer, but they hadn't gone much in the last few years, and it was Gray who always argued that it was a question of expense. It was different for Cam and Harriet, he said; they didn't have children to save for.

They all went into the kitchen now, and Cam said grimly, "Yeah, we found out something about the other half too. We left early because the night got shot to hell."

"He's been swearing all the way from Williston," said Harriet. "Cam, please don't dump this on Astrid tonight." She was really disturbed.

"Oh, come on," said Astrid. "As long as you haven't come to tell me Gray's dead, you might as well talk. I'll make us some coffee."

Harriet sat down in the rocking chair, sighed, and looked at the ceiling. Cam propped a foot on the stove hearth. "Well, we were at the Willis Inn, and who comes in now but my now famous brother and his girl friend, both of them fixed up like Beautiful People, and Lolita looking all of fourteen."

"*I* wanted to leave then," said Harriet, "but Cam wouldn't."

"You're damn right I wouldn't. I wanted to meet him face to face and shake him up a bit, but hell, we couldn't get near them. Steering Harriet was like trying to dance with a tank."

"You didn't really think I was going to let you get near them and start something, did you?"

He narrowed his eyes at her and she tilted her chin pertly. "Yeah," said Cam. "Well, I finally left her at our table and started around the floor while she was holding her breath and crossing her fingers in case we started something that would hit the papers and slam old Fletch between the eyes. And guess who got there before me. George Rollins. There he was, leaning over their table talking to Gray in this polite, confidential way, and Baby Doll was getting bigger-eyed by the second. Then George went out to the lobby, and Gray got up and motioned her to come, and she sat back harder in the chair, looking sulky. But he just stood there waiting. She got up and went out hanging onto his arm with both hands and talking fast."

"Saying, 'Don't believe him, it wasn't that way at all!' " said Astrid.

"You know something I don't know?" Cam asked.

"Go on with the story."

"I never found out what it was about. I tried to look into the lobby without being spotted. They were over by the main door with George talking, and she was still hanging onto Gray and snuffling into his handkerchief, and he was looking old enough to be her father. Then they went out. So I don't know what's going on, but that's not what I came around to tell you."

"Oh, God, can there be more?" said Astrid.

"Yes. Listen, you've got to dump him. . . . He's my brother, and I guess I love him, even though I felt like driving my fist into his face tonight when he showed up in there all gussied up with that little slut. But we care about you too, damn it. So you get that divorce started, and we'll be your witnesses."

When she didn't answer, but stared down at her cup, he leaned across the table and said urgently, "He's sure of you, Astrid. If the thing blows up in his face you'll still

be here like Mother, ready to welcome home the wandering boy, no questions asked. Well, he doesn't deserve that.
What he deserves is Dorri, and the sooner he's got her
slung legally around his neck like the albatross, the better.
If anything's going to save his soul, which Fletch worries
and prays about, there's an ordeal that ought to do it." He
sat back, winded. "There, by God, I've said it."

"And you're glad," said Astrid.

"You mad with me?"

She shook her head, trying to smile. "How could I be?
You two and Fletch and Nora are my family. So I'll tell
you what George wanted with them tonight."

When she finished, Cam whistled. "Good God! He *is*
over the edge. Buying a job like that! And letting her
drive it."

"He probably didn't know she'd driven it until George
told him," said Astrid.

"Have you checked your bank balance lately?" Harriet
asked.

Astrid nodded. "Yes, and I've taken care of it."

"But you don't intend to take my advice, do you?" Cam
said. "I can tell. Never mind, I had my say, and if my wife
says 'I told you so,' I may make her walk home."

"I'm scared he's ruined your night's sleep." Harriet said
to Astrid. "Talk about women not keeping anything to
themselves! Cam can't keep a thing bottled up."

"That's what makes me such a passionate lover," said
Cam complacently. Harriet gave him a sidewise look, and
her mouth tilted up in a funny little smile. It was this,
more than anything else, that was going to ruin Astrid's
sleep tonight.

# Chapter 12

In the morning George Rollins stopped in at the wharf while he was hauling. Still tactful, he told her he'd seen Dorri but not where. "Took me some time to locate her, but finally I saw the car parked, so I went looking. She's got no license, not even a learner's permit. The owner didn't know she'd been taking the car out; he'd had to go on some business errands, and she took it then. I told him she'd been making a nuisance of herself, in addition to illegal driving." He stopped and lit a cigarette. "He promised it wouldn't happen again, and I let them off with a warning. I hope that's all right with you."

"Of course it is. I'm not out for blood, George. I just don't want that going on in my driveway."

The boys had been standing beside their mother, solemnly gazing down into the boat. "Hi, men!" he saluted them. "How about a ride around the cove?"

They couldn't speak for rapture; they waved to their mother as if they were setting out for Europe. They found their tongues before the circuit was made, and when he returned them to the wharf they were both talking at once, and both were helping to steer. He handed them up one at a time to Astrid.

"Thanks, George," she said. "They'll talk about this all day."

"Beats me, the things some people do," he said. "I'll never get over being surprised. I'll tell you one thing, it'd take a hell of a pull to get me away from something like *that*." He nodded toward the boys. "So long, men," he said to them.

"Thank you, Mr. Rollins," Peter sang out without having to be told, and Chris echoed him.

Dinah called and suggested a trip into the countryside behind Limerock to visit her sister's farm for the day. Astrid was glad to go, to get the poison of the last week out of her system. She'd visited the farm before and knew it was like another world up there in the hills.

The children were boisterous from their boat ride and with this expedition ahead of them. She sent them up to tidy their room just to keep them out from under foot while she put a lunch together. The telephone rang again, and she thought it was Dinah to add or ask something.

"*Astrid.*" It was Gray's voice. She was so astonished it took the stiffening out of her legs and she groped backward for a chair. She couldn't help sounding out of breath.

"Yes. What is it? Where are you calling from?"

"The main house." Then he didn't want Dorri to hear; but that needn't mean anything. She was through with believing in signs. "Look, Astrid, I know you've been bothered lately. I didn't have a chance to apologize about the telephone, but I am now and about the car."

She couldn't think of anything to say; she just sat there

holding the phone tightly, straining to hear something else even though he was waiting for her to speak.

"Astrid, are you still there?" he asked with a familiar quick impatience.

"Yes."

"Can't you say something?"

"What?" she asked politely. "There's nothing *to* say. Oh yes, I..." She fumbled hazily for the words. "I thought you might come and see the boys. If you could come alone, I mean, as if you'd taken a day off this far-away job you're on. Or you could write them if you can't come alone." She waited, heard no answer, fumbled on. "Would you like to talk to them now?"

"No!" he exclaimed. "I mean—I'd want to take time with them, and I can't right now." Because you're afraid of what they might ask you, she told him, and Dorri might come barging in on you. "But I'd like to see them. Look, I'll get back to you on that, and we'll fix something up." His voice dropped even lower. "I miss them like hell. I love them, Astrid, no matter what—"

Behind him Dorri's voice rang across the unseen room. "*There* you are, sweetie!"

Astrid hung up. She knew now they could never have five minutes alone to settle anything, unless he bound and gagged Dorri and put her in a closet first. She went back to packing a lunch, keeping her mind within rigid boundaries. When Dinah came and they drove up into the highlands, she had a weird sense of escape, as if the house itself had become a menacing presence whose voice was the telephone, giving commands, rewards, and punishments.

At the farm there was a blossoming orchard, lambs, calves, foals. The property included a large pond, with a cottage beside it that was rented in summer. Today they used it for their headquarters rather than have the children running in and out of the main house. There were frogs in the pond, and Peter would have spent his whole day trying to establish diplomatic relations with at least one if pony rides and the baby animals hadn't been so fascinating.

If Dinah's family knew about Astrid's difficulties, they didn't show it. The entire day was as far removed from the trouble as if it had never occurred. In the late afternoon, after he'd finished hauling, Ben drove up, and there was a farmhouse supper with baked beans, salads, hot johnnycake. Astrid hated to go home. It had always been a delight to return to the house, but now she felt it to be unsafe, and it was the most threatening when it was the quietest.

Dinah's children had gone home in the pick-up with their father. She and Dinah carried in the sleeping boys, undressed them and settled them in bed. She hated to have Dinah leave, but, fighting these strange imaginings of hers, she was too proud to ask anything; it was Dinah who said, "Hey, let me stay a half hour or so and have a cup of tea? Ben'll see the kids in and out of the bathtub and into bed. I feel as if I'd been running a race all day."

By the time they'd finished their tea, not having much to say but peaceful in their stillness, the house seemed to have slid gradually back into itself again.

Sunday was Children's Day and she attended the special service. Peter sang "Jesus Loves Me" in his clear, vigorous young voice. The sun came in on his yellow head. Astrid hardened herself against easy sentimental tears but heard some surreptitious nose-blowing around her.

Chris was one of a group of smiling or tearful three-year-olds who "spoke a piece" together. It was all of four lines long. She was happy to see that Chris was one of the cheerful performers. At the end of the concert each child received a blossoming geranium. Peter said, "Thank you," but in the car he said to her critically, "Why don't they give out good things like kittens or frogs?"

"Because everybody wouldn't take good care of a kitten or a frog."

"How do they know everybody will take good care of a flower?"

"They don't," she said, "but it can't suffer like a living thing." Some people said plants did suffer, but that was too deep a subject—maybe not for Peter, but certainly for her this morning. Anyway, she had never let the children willfully destroy growing things, so her conscience was clear.

Chris adored his pink geranium and kept smelling it all the way to Cam's. Two of the Price sisters were home from far parts, and there was a large family gathering, with enough children so that Peter was willing to let the imponderables go for a while. Chris didn't want to get far from his geranium or his mother, until a ten-year-old girl cousin took him over.

On Monday afternoon she went to Williston to get a graduation gift and cards for Kevin. The boys began clamoring for ice-cream cones the instant she drove into an empty slot in front of the drugstore.

"No cones in the car," she said. "When we get home you can have cones." She went into the gift shop next to the drugstore and picked out cards and a pair of sturdy wooden bookends, weighted with polished beach rocks. Then she went to the drugstore for a few items. When she came out Dorri was leaning into the car talking animatedly to two entranced small boys. But Chris wasn't so entranced that he didn't see Astrid; he was always on the watch for her.

"Hi, Mama!" he called past Dorri's ear.

Dorri turned, smiling. "Hi, Astrid." Her motions were leisurely with self-confidence, as if she had never screamed suicide in the bathroom. She shook back the lustrous curtains of hair. "How are you?"

"Mama!" Peter shouted. "Dorri says her and Daddy's going to give us ponies!"

"And a dog," added Chris. He barked realistically, starting up a terrier in the next car.

Astrid didn't speak but kept on toward the car. At the last possible moment Dorri moved nonchalantly away from the door, her smile unchanging. Now Astrid wondered why she had not seen it all there before in the triangular little face, that sly, complacent malice. "You're looking a little older," Dorri observed. "You can't keep this up forever, you know. Sooner or later it'll get to you." She leaned back decoratively against the trunk of the next car, and the terrier inside was furious at her boldness.

Of the people passing on the broad sidewalk behind them, or driving by outside the parked car, it was likely that some of them knew either Astrid or Dorri or both and saw them in this confrontation. Astrid didn't know or care. She was only concerned with her own reactions and

how well she handled them. She went around to the driver's side and started to get in.

"Are we getting ponies, Mama?" Peter cried piercingly.

"Yes, you are," Dorri said from the other side. "When
you come to visit your daddy and me." She held up her
left hand. "You see this pretty diamond ring? It means
your daddy's going to marry me."

Astrid put her package on the seat and shut her door
without slamming it. "You boys be good, and don't touch
that bag," she said calmly. "I'm going to walk Dorri to her
car." She went around the back of hers, and Dorri's smiling insolence turned to instant alarm. She almost scurried
between the two cars toward the sidewalk, head swinging
this way and that. Astrid followed. Dorri looked back
quickly; she was pale, her eyes staring.

"Come along," Astrid said in a pleasant and authorita-
tive voice. "We need to talk, but not in front of the boys."

"I came with Mavis, and she's parked way back there
by the Red and White." Her mouth was unsteady.

"The walk will give us a good chance to talk. You
needn't worry, Dorri. What I have to say won't be full
of dirty words." Dorri, unmoving, tossed a glance in the
other direction from the Red and White. Her lipstick
stood out like paint. "Are you anemic?" Astrid asked her.
"You've no color at all."

Dorri was so obviously trying not to look the other way
that Astrid did look and saw Gray coming out of the
hardware store with a carton. At the same time a small
van backed out and revealed the green Audi.

"Oh!" cried Astrid as if in delight and surprise. "Let's
go that way!" She tucked her hand inside Dorri's rigid
elbow and started her moving. Afterward she remembered

meeting a couple of astonished stares but couldn't remember to whom they belonged.

Almost there, Dorri broke loose and ran to the car. Gray was putting the carton in the trunk. He shut down the lid, and as he did so Dorri threw herself at him, gasping, "Gray *darling!*"

Almost knocked off balance by the attack, and half laughing with embarrassment, he looked around to see who was watching. He saw Astrid standing on the sidewalk. His dark face went immobile, but he couldn't prevent the blush. He disengaged himself from the embrace, but kept an arm around Dorri like a gesture of defiance.

"Hello, Astrid," he said in a low voice.

"Hello, Gray." She stepped off the curb and went close to them.

"I didn't do *anything*, Gray!" Dorri wailed. "Right out of a clear sky she—"

"Hush." He kept his eyes on Astrid. "Well?"

"Maybe you'd like to come over to the car," she said softly, "and confirm what Dorri's just told the boys. My story's been knocked into a cocked hat. Now that you've made a liar out of me, I'm afraid you'll have to straighten things out with them."

"I don't want to see them," he said. "I don't know what to say. Not while everything's up in the air like this. It would be too confusing, they could never understand."

"They could understand if she'd stop being so damn selfish!" Dorri exclaimed. "Then it would straighten out all right."

"Be quiet," said Gray.

"Well, I'm tired of all this crap. Why can't she leave us alone?"

"I said, *Be quiet.*" He wasn't raising his voice any more than Astrid was. On the sidewalk nobody was rude enough to stand still and listen, but they certainly saw, and they had heard Dorri. Astrid, watching Gray's face under the new forelock, was both compassionate and grimly amused.

"Astrid and I will work this out, Dorri," he said. "But not on Main Street. Get into the car." He turned her toward the car door and reached for the handle. She broke loose from him and screamed something at Astrid. Only one phrase was intelligible, but vividly so, like the sign that accompanied it.

Astrid had one glimpse of Gray's shock and dismay, but by then she was already on the move without consciously knowing it; Dorri's throat was strained back under her left hand, a pulse throbbing hard under her pressing thumb. She pushed the girl against the car and looked into the bulging and terrified eyes. She felt she could keep it up forever.

"Astrid—for God's sake!" Gray was trying to get her hand away from Dorri's throat. "People are looking! Are you crazy? You're *strangling* her!"

"Oh, bug off, Gray," she said, smiling. She released the pressure slightly and with her right hand she slapped Dorri's face as hard as she could.

At once that side flamed as violently as if it had been seared. In the silence before Dorri could get her breath, Astrid said, "Really, Gray, you should wash her mouth out with soap and water at least once a day."

She walked away without looking back or seeing anyone else on the sidewalk, entirely satisfied by the burning tingle in her hand and the memory of the companion fire on the girl's face.

The line of parked cars and pick-ups between her car and the Audi had hidden it all from the boys, and besides, Kevin was there, leaning over the door and letting the boys both talk at once. She stood on the sidewalk watching and listening, taking some deep breaths. She knew she could easily start to tremble, and that would never do.

"It was *this* big!" Peter was measuring.

"No, no!" Chris shouted. "*This* big!" He stretched his arms as wide as he could.

"Weren't you scared?" Kevin asked in awe. She stepped down off the curb. "Hi, Mama!" the boys yelled, rowdy boys now, telling tall tales and drunk with their own powers of invention.

Kevin straightened up. "I saw it," he said. "I was in the bank." She became aware for the first time that school was out, and she wondered without real concern how many of Dorri's contemporaries had also seen. Kevin was saying, "Somebody told me she'd been at this car first."

"Who? What?" She smiled at him. "Chris's monster?"

He tried to grin in response. "Yeah. Well, I tried to get them thinking about something else."

"I appreciate that."

He stepped out toward the street and tensely watched something she couldn't see. She got into the car. The boys tumbled about the back seat like puppies, giggling and crying "ouch" with dramatic emphasis. Kevin came around to her door, saying, "They've gone. Want me to drive you home? I can get a ride back to pick up my own car."

"Gosh, no, I'm fine."

"You sure?"

"Positive! I think it did me good." She tried to sound

jaunty. "Of course I'll probably be arrested for assault and battery and get the Prices into the paper after all."

"He wouldn't let her. He's not that numb." Kevin blushed. "Excuse me. I know you don't want anybody putting him down, but—oh, listen, Astrid, there's nothing that'll turn him against her as long as she keeps telling him she's crazy about him. *I know*."

She looked with pity into his young eyes, which seemed as vulnerable as Peter's or Chris's. "I know. At least I'm beginning to know."

# Chapter
# 13

She got the chuckling, wriggling children into their restraints, thankful for every moment that passed without Peter's asking her about Dorri and Daddy. The word "marry" meant nothing to him; all that mattered was that Dorri'd brought a message from Daddy, and it concerned ponies.

There was a dangerous interlude when they passed the Lowell pasture. The children yelled, "Hi, Bianca! Hi, Ralph! Hi, Elfie!" It was hard on her ears, but not on her heart, because they didn't instantly ask her about *their* ponies.

By the time she reached the house she was having the inevitable bad reaction—the letdown from the tremendous burst of energy, and the shame. She fixed the ice-cream cones for the boys; she took two aspirins and sipped tea, tried to calm herself, and after a while she felt less shaky and could see one fact very clearly. She had to get away for a while.

What she had done on Main Street had been satisfying at the time. In retrospect it was frightening. Up until then she had been in control, even when she felt the worst. . . . She remembered the girl's throat under her hand, the frantic pulse beating under her thumb, and the memory made her sick enough to throw up the tea. She remembered Gray's struggle to loosen her grip, and her stomach went on having spasms when there was nothing left to come up.

"I lost control," she said to the sweating face reflected in the bathroom mirror. "I could have done anything, and I wouldn't have cared!"

She washed her face in cold water and went out and called Dinah. "Do you think Emily would rent me the cottage for a couple of weeks, starting now?" she asked. "We'd stay out of everybody's way."

"I'll call her, but I'm so sure of it you can start packing now. What really happened on Main Street today?"

"Oh, for heaven's sake, Dine! I've only been home about a half hour!"

"The grapevine's very fast, but the stuff loses something in the translation, as they say."

Astrid's stomach contracted again. "I don't want to talk about it right now. The kids are coming in," she lied.

"I'll come over tonight then, after I talk with Em."

They ate their supper on the shore and she let the boys play until sunset so they would be good and tired. They were yawning and heavy-footed when they returned to the house, and Chris was dozing by the time she kissed him good night. But when she leaned over Peter, he whispered, "Be sure you lock all the doors tonight!"

"I always do, so a sudden gust of wind won't blow them open. A raccoon might come in and eat all our doughnuts," she joked.

This possibility didn't thrill Peter as it usually did. "But something else might happen," he went on whispering.

"What, Peter?"

"*Something.*" In the dusk his wide eyes looked black. "Robbers, maybe."

She wondered if he'd overheard talk about the Cades in spite of her caution. She said in a soft, easy way, "Sometimes people go into somebody else's house when nobody's home, and they steal things, like the television or some nice old clock—oh, anything they think they can sell and get money for."

"They're bad people."

"Yes. You know it's wrong to take what isn't yours, even if it's only some little thing."

"How little?"

"Oh, something from the garden. Or a nickel from a pocketbook. A hammer. A toy boat. *Anything* that belongs to somebody else. But these people only come into the house when the owners are away. I don't worry about it one bit, Peter, and if I don't worry, you shouldn't."

"I won't," he promised, still in a whisper, "but don't forget to lock the doors."

"I shan't." She went downstairs hoping his sudden fear of burglars wasn't really a mask for deeper, wounding worries. That damned little wretch! she thought with fresh fury. I hope I scared the hell out of her and Gray too. I wish I'd given him a good swift kick while I was in the mood. *Numb* is the right word, Kevin—

"Oh Lord!" she said out loud. "The Cades. Vandalism and burglary in *my* house, *my* garden?"

Her life had already been vandalized enough to do her for a lifetime. She would have to have a house-sitter. George could check the house regularly, of course, but he couldn't be everywhere at once. Perhaps she could get Kevin, if his parents would allow it. He needed only to sleep in the house to show it was occupied, and he didn't travel with a crowd that would be likely to move in on him loaded with liquor and pot.

She made hopeful plans for him to occupy the spare room, even though she couldn't ask him until she was sure of the cottage.

Dinah drove in with good news from her sister. The rent was extremely modest, because the cottage would have been empty until the first of July anyway. Emily liked her and the children; they could move in tomorrow if they liked.

There was plenty left unsaid. Astrid guessed that Emily had heard the whole story from Dinah, and the two sisters were taking her on as a worthy cause, but she was too desperate now to let pride stand in her way.

"If I can get Kevin for a house-sitter, we'll be sleeping there tomorrow night," she said.

"Poor Kevin," said Dinah. "Going away to college this fall will be the best thing that can happen to him right now. Are you going to tell your best friend what happened today, or do I have to go by the lurid reports?"

"*Lurid.*" Astrid groaned. "I'll bet. Well, it *was* lurid, whatever that word really means." She told the story as briefly as possible. "There. I felt murderous, Dinah, and that's why I have to go away from this place for a while and try to get myself all together."

With unusual diffidence Dinah asked, "Don't you think you'd feel better if you started a divorce? If something happened in the meantime, like Gray suddenly coming to his senses, you wouldn't have to go through with it."

"I don't know," said Astrid. "I don't know." An ache was beginning in her neck and the back of her head.

Dinah said quickly, "You poor thing, you get up there and try to forget it all for a while. I know that's really impossible, but out of sight, out of mind. And maybe everything will come clear all at once." She snapped her fingers.

Fletch's pick-up drove in. "They've heard it too," muttered Astrid. "Poor Fletch. This has all put years on him."

"I'll go." Dinah gave Astrid a hug and a kiss. She spoke to Nora in passing, and then stopped to ask Fletch something, which gave Astrid a chance to speak alone to Nora.

"Fletch must think I've let the family down. I gave in to temptation."

"Who's got a better right?" Nora asked belligerently. "Way I heard it, she deserved a lot more."

"And he did too, Nora. He's as bad as her parents are for letting her get away with things. I wonder what he'll give her this time for a present."

"This time?" Fletch was coming in.

It had been a slip; nobody else knew about the phone calls. She said, "Well, he must have had to promise something to dry her tears."

"What can follow an Audi?" Fletch asked. His tired, affectionate smile made her want to cry. In a stammering rush she confessed the whole story of the afternoon. Nora listened, nodding at intervals, her strong broad face lively with sympathetic excitement. Fletch had taken off his glasses, and his somber attention made her feel like a child sent to the principal's office.

"I'm sorry if you're ashamed of me, Fletch," she finished defiantly. "But she had no right talking to the children about herself and Gray. When she finally broke loose on me, I forgot myself." She remembered again the strong wild throbbing under her thumb. It had an unwelcome fascination for her.

"You had plenty of provocation. Personally, I can turn the other cheek just so many times. But Gray's the one I'm concerned with. It's like seeing him struggling in the water, drowning, and I can't reach him but I have to keep on trying because maybe—if we can just touch fingertips—I can save him."

"How—if he doesn't want to be saved?"

"I don't know. I only know that it has to *be*. 'Can a man take fire in his bosom, and his clothes not be burned?' " he asked quietly. " 'Can one go upon hot coals and his feet be not burned? . . . Whosoever committed adultery with a woman lacks understanding, he destroys his own soul.' "

The skin tightened on the back of Astrid's head, a chill ran along her arms. Nora said matter-of-factly, "Prayer's supposed to move mountains, but Gray's in a class by himself. What I think is that *she'll* do it, in time."

"We never know how our prayers will be answered," said Fletch. "If you can just hold together, Astrid, and you can! You have the strength."

"Today I've got serious doubts about that. So I'm going away for two weeks, up to Dinah's sister's farm in Parmenter. I can think more clearly then, I hope."

They were both nodding in approval, Nora with a smile, Fletch solemn and kind. "I'm hoping to get Kevin to sleep here nights, but of course I'll call George too. If I can't get Kevin—well, I'll go anyway. I *have* to." Her hands were locked painfully in her lap. And I won't have to talk about Gray with anyone for all that time, she thought, craving the release. Daddy, the man who builds houses far from home, isn't the same man who's walking on hot coals and carrying fire in his bosom. I can talk about the kids' Gray without scorching my tongue and almost believe what I say.

"There's a frog pond," she said aloud.

Fletch laughed. "Peter told me once he wanted to be a frog because they jump so far. And then he sang me some of this song about a frog."

"It's his favorite right now. I'd like to get him onto something else before he realizes the sad ending. Maybe we can learn some new ones while we're away."

"I'd promise that we'll pray for good weather," said Nora, "except Fletch considers that a form of nagging." They all three laughed, comfortable together with Fletch's faith. When they were leaving, she asked them to keep her whereabouts a secret from Gray.

"I don't suppose he'll ask, but if he did try to call me for any reason and couldn't locate us, it might do some good." She shrugged in self-ridicule.

"Sure it'll do some good," Fletch said warmly. "We'll get him back yet, and maybe save that child's soul into the bargain."

She wanted to call Kevin, but with her newly eroded self-confidence she couldn't make up her mind. If either parent answered, how would they respond to her request to speak to Kevin? Even though he said they understood, she wasn't sure that they approved; they might be extra-sensitive to the fear of scandal because Kevin had become involved in enough of that already. And if she spoke frankly, like one parent to another even though she was much younger, and asked if Kevin could house-sit for her, Kevin might never forgive her for treating him like a child.

She tried to think she didn't care, but she did. She was about to give up and take a chance on the Cades visiting the house between George's checks when Kevin drove in. It was nearly ten o'clock.

"You must be psychic," she said.

"No," he said seriously. "We just got through our baseball dinner and were sitting around yakking, and I got to wondering how you were feeling after this afternoon."

"In need of a house-sitter for two weeks," she said. "Would you be interested? You'd only have to be here to sleep, and I'd leave plenty on hand for you to have all the snacks you wanted and a good breakfast."

"To sleep! Heck—I'd spend my whole evenings here, just to get away from that tribe of siblings! Where are you going?"

"I'll tell you, in case you have to get in touch for some reason, but I don't want Gray to know. Is that understood?"

"Understood," he said grimly. "Look, I'll keep the lawn mowed, I'll tend the garden—"

"The garden won't need any attention for a while yet—it's barely started—but the lawn grows like mad this time of year. It's all yours. What about your parents?"

"What about them?" He looked surprised.

"I want them to approve."

"I'm eighteen, I earn my own money for my clothes. I'll do my chores at home, I'll be behaving myself. What more could they ask?"

She laughed, thinking, A great deal, Kevin, but we won't go into that.

# Chapter
# 14

**S**he wrapped the bookends, helped the children to print their names on one card and signed the other one, and left everything on the kitchen table for Kevin to find when he came.

If distance didn't lend enchantment to the view, at least it was distance. It was a relief to be away from the telephone calls, well-meaning or otherwise, and from surprise encounters; she lived a gentle nursery routine with the children, eating outdoors, visiting the animals every day, taking long walks in the woods or around the pond. The teen-agers on the farm were good to the children, giving them pony and donkey rides.

Chris was in love with a donkey foal which seemed to requite his affections. Peter slept without bad dreams; once he awoke ecstatic about having been a frog. "And wow, could I *jump!*"

She herself slept well most nights; she was too tired to do otherwise. They had come on a Tuesday, and on the next Monday morning she awoke with the positive conviction that she and Gray should be able to talk alone together sensibly by now. He might even be anxious for such a talk, and today was the day. She was sure of it. She had dreamed, just before daylight, of sleeping with him and of their turning to each other to make love.

She couldn't leave the children at the farm for someone else to look after, so they walked up to the main house after breakfast, and while the children helped to feed the hens she called Dinah and asked if she could leave the boys with her while she did a number of errands and kept some appointments.

The boys didn't want to leave their various loves, until she mentioned Poochie. She went straight to Dinah's and had a second breakfast, without telling her the real reason for the trip home. She'd brought her washing and vaguely mentioned doing things in Limerock. Dinah didn't ask questions, which meant she suspected one of the things might be a visit to a lawyer. Astrid went around to her own house half dreading it, yet still under the influence of her dream. She couldn't understand why its aura had been affirmative rather than negative; in the early days of Gray's desertion, if she dreamed of him she would wake crying, or numbingly depressed, which was worse.

No, it had to be because this was the right time to talk. She'd handle it perfectly and Gray would thus respond. . . . She walked down over newly shorn lawn to her garden and saw that it was growing well; she remembered suddenly that she'd planned to get some tomato plants that day in Williston. Oh well, she might find some even better ones upcountry to bring home with her.

She let herself into the house. It was tidy except for Kevin's breakfast dishes in the sink. Her mail was stacked on the washer. She sorted it quickly, then she started her washing and went upstairs to look around. His bed was made in the spare room; there was an open book on the nightstand. The cards from her and the boys were standing on the chest of drawers, and so were the bookends, with a few books from downstairs between them.

She was touched by the arrangement. He must have had other cards and gifts at home, but these he kept with him, as if they belonged here. She was impressed too by his neatness. He'd had no way of knowing she'd be dropping in today, yet everything was in its place; there was no clutter even in the living room, except for the open *TV Guide* on the arm of the sofa.

The June day was approaching its zenith of heat and brilliance when she hung out her washing. Then she drove up to Williston and down the river on the other side and out to Partridge Point. When she reached the tarmac parking area, it was nearly high tide; the salt river was all a pale-blue glitter, flowing up to the woods and the flowering fields. There was no wind but a hot, shimmering, aromatic silence in which even the birds seemed subdued.

The Audi and the pick-up were in front of the garage. Windows were open in the main house and in the flat, but she heard no human sounds. She walked past the front of the house to the new wing to see if he was there—Dorri could have been lying out in the sun somewhere. It would make everything ideally simple if she was out of earshot. Astrid planned to ask Gray to come with her somewhere for a private talk, even if it was no farther than a half mile up the road.

But Gray wasn't in the new wing. She called, knowing even before she lifted her voice that no one would answer. She walked behind the house past sheltered lawns and

banks of perennials, around the garage, and up the steps
to the balcony.

Watch it, she warned herself sardonically. They might
be having a noon special. Maybe you'd better leave now.
But nobody seemed to be in the flat. From the balcony she
could look toward the shore, over mown grass to a steep
field sparkling with daisies and fringed with spruces. Beyond their dark boughs the river sparkled blindingly. She
thought she heard faraway cries, separate from those of a
few gulls crossing the blue-white sky of a hot noon. The
lovers were probably having a swim, and if they thought
they were alone in the world, and skinny-dipping, her arrival wouldn't put Gray in a very cooperative mood.

She waited a little while, looking at the flowers, walking
through the new wing, handling tools which Gray had
handled; she was meditative rather than sad and still optimistic. But when they hadn't come in half an hour, she
felt that she'd lost the initiative. Her earlier sense of sure-
footedness was going fast.

She wrote a note on the pad she kept in the glove com-
partment. "Dear Gray: I'll be at the house this afternoon.
Will you please call me there before four? It's very important—" she hesitated, then added mendaciously—"to
all three of us. As ever—A." If Dorri thought she was
ready to talk divorce, she wouldn't try to prevent a meeting.

She went upstairs to the flat and set the paper against
the sugar bowl, with the salt and pepper shakers to hold
it in place. When she drove away, she felt enervated. Anything had seemed possible when she awoke this morning,
but now conviction had drained away as the tide would
later drain from the river, leaving an expanse of flats.

At home she made soup from the contents of a one-cup envelope, ate some saltines with it, and read a letter from her mother, who was rehearsing for summer opera in Wisconsin. "Why don't you write?" she scolded. Astrid hadn't written her since the trouble began, and now she jotted down a rough draft of a note that wouldn't exactly lie but wouldn't give anything away, either. She could always fill it up with the children's doings and sayings.

She went out to get the clothes, and on her way in she heard the telephone ringing. She was so excited she tripped on the threshold and nearly fell in through the door, her clothesbasket flying ahead of her and landing upside down. So tense and out of breath she could hardly speak, she reached the telephone. It was a woman who wanted her to bake for the church fair in July; and did she have anything for the Attic Sale?

"I'll look," said Astrid hoarsely.

Slowly she gathered up her spilled laundry and smoothed and folded it with automatic gestures. She wished she'd gone down to the river and spoken to him, even at the risk of catching him playing nymphs and satyrs with Dorri. She hated staying in the house now; she wanted to be gone. But there were two and a half hours until four, so she had to wait. She washed her dishes and Kevin's; she tried to put her mind on a contribution to the Attic Sale, but didn't want to go into the attic for fear of being too far from the telephone. But she didn't have to find something now, she thought distractedly. It was only the first week in June.

It was Graduation Day at Williston High, Dinah had reminded her this morning. With nothing else to do, she worried about tonight. It was traditional for the graduates to have an all-night shore picnic after the exercises, and if Kevin went, the house would be left alone. Should she call George about that, or leave a note for Kevin to do it? What if Kevin didn't come back here at all today before the exercises? Finally she called George herself and told him the problem. He was laid up with a sprained back, but he'd ask the sheriff's patrol to swing around and check the house. She thanked him, feeling only slightly relieved and knowing the real anxiety wasn't about the house. It was past four now, and Gray hadn't called.

She had to go and pick up the boys; Dinah and Ben were going to the graduation that night because Ben was on the school board. First she called Nora.

"I'm just saying hello and we're all fine. I had to come home to do a few things, but I'm on my way back now." She tried to sound breezy, not as wiped out as she felt.

"You didn't see Gray, by any chance?" asked Nora.

"No, and not on purpose, either. I went across the river to see him but he wasn't there, so I left a note."

"Oh dear," said Nora. "What if she sees it first and destroys it?"

"I made it sound as if I was ready to talk about divorce, so I'm pretty sure she won't hide it. But he hasn't called, so I guess he's not in the mood," she said flippantly. "Perhaps he'd rather hear from my lawyer."

"*Did* you want to talk divorce?"

"No," said Astrid. "Just to talk like the two human beings we used to be, who could always talk over things. There are a lot of facts I want to know. Maybe he'd *like* me to hold off a while—well, I thought that, but he hasn't called, so maybe I don't think it any more." Her voice faded from weariness.

"Listen, honey," Nora said, "Fletch and I went to the movies in Limerock two nights ago—at last they got something Fletch could sit through without blushing—and who'd we meet on the sidewalk outside but Gray and his Sunbonnet Baby. She had this insolent little grin I'd have loved to wipe off, and Gray had his mouth set like a steel trap, defying us to say a word. And I didn't, if you can believe it." She laughed. "Probably surprised Gray. It did me. Well, Fletch stopped. He managed not to let go on them like a reincarnation of old Huw ap Rice preaching on sin, but he told Gray that his behavior had driven his wife and sons away from home. *That* brought Gray up with a round turn. He wanted to know where you were, but Fletch wouldn't tell him. He just took my arm and walked me to the car."

If that had disturbed Gray, why hadn't he called now? Because he saw no way of talking with her without Dorri's presence? Because he was angry and determined enough now to want to hear from her lawyer, not her?

"... Been some worked up ever since," Nora was saying. "He's been walking at night—miles, I guess. He's gone for hours, I know that. Now he's not home from work yet, and he should be. But he gets mulling on things, and he can't talk to Cam, you know how Cam feels about all this. So Fletch has to try to calm himself down before he comes back to the kids and me."

"I don't want Fletch so upset, damn it!" Astrid cried angrily.

"He can't help it. Gray's his little brother. He was looking over old snapshots the other day, sighing and shaking his head."

"He's got to stop thinking of that little boy. Gray's

grown up, he's responsible for himself now. Nobody else is." She felt furious enough to fly, at least to run away from them all.

"I try to pound that into Fletch's head, but he's as set in his way as Gray in his. Cam's just as bad. Well, the young ones are showing up, so I'll let you go. We love you, dear."

"I love you too, Nora," she said, ashamed. "And tell Fletch from me—no, never mind. I know he can't be any different. I just hate to have him wearing himself out for nothing."

"If he succeeds in saving Gray, it won't be for nothing." Nora's serenity reproved her. "And who knows? That might be the saving of the child too."

Yes, a truly good person would think of that. But I am not a truly good person, Astrid thought. She went around and picked up the children, promising Dinah whole days and nights of child-sitting in return. All four children and Poochie were now quiescent after their strenuous day on the shore, and Astrid's two fell asleep in the car before they reached the farm.

The cottage in the hills was a refuge Astrid dreaded leaving. The first week had been rich and spacious; the second rushed her. Halfway through it Dinah called and left word for her to call back. "Nothing wrong," Emily assured her. "Just something she wanted to tell you."

Astrid wished she could avoid calling; she was tired of being told things people thought she should know.

"Hi!" Dinah was ebullient. "Nobody's dead or anything, and I could've save this for you, but I thought you might want to know now. It looks as if Bonny and Clyde have left town."

So that's my answer, Astrid thought. She had to sit down. "Are you all right?" Dinah inquired.

"Yes, fine. No, *fine*'s not the exact word, but I'm all in one piece. Thanks, Dine. I'm glad you prepared me for it." She was, really, though *glad* wasn't the exact word, either. "Tell me the rest."

"Well, it comes from Carrie. They stopped in there, last Monday sometime—the same day you were down—and the Princess picked up some clothes. *She* was her sweet bubbly self, but *he* didn't have anything to say, not that Carrie would give him a chance. But even Baby Dear didn't say anything about their going somewhere. Maybe they're afraid of the Mann Act or something. Well, Carrie got one of her premonitions, after twenty-four hours went by without a telephone call and nobody answered at Partridge Point, so she and Rupe drove over there yesterday."

Astrid consciously loosened her grip on the telephone. Her knees were shaking. She was watching them, fascinated. "Then what?" Her chin felt shaky too.

"The place was all locked up. His pick-up was gone, the car was gone, there were no tools left around the new wing; everything was in order. They looked in the windows of the flat and couldn't see even a sweater or a shirt left there."

"Well," said Astrid. "Interesting, isn't it?" He's running away from my note. Where? Why?

"Carrie says Rupe's all to pieces, but she's so glad to be rid of that kid she can't hide it. The way she keeps moaning on, about how if her darling was ever found dead in a ditch she'd never forgive herself, makes me wonder how much she wishes it would happen."

"Poor Carrie, sometimes I'm sorry for her."

"Maybe I should feel that way too, but we can't all be true Christians like Fletch, can we? I feel worse for Rupe. Will you finish out your week there?"

"Yes, I wouldn't attempt to pry these kids loose yet. They're either soggy from playing around the frog pond, or they smell like lambs, donkeys, ponies, you name it. *De-wicious!* Chris says."

She marveled at the lightness, even the merriment, of her voice, and wondered if Dinah thought she was slightly cracked. For the rest of her time at the farm she had this curious lightheadedness, not like the onset of a sickness, and she slept heavily at night. Finally she recognized it as relief in its purest essence, like oxygen to the lung-sufferer. For the first time she faced the possibility of divorce. It took some doing to get enough courage to look the monster in the eye, but it wasn't too bad. After all, she'd already confronted the preliminary facts. The boy she'd loved, the man she'd married (with whom their bed had been their space ship, their secret island), the boys' father —they'd all existed, but no longer.

She was now more often annoyed or scornful rather than yearning. When she dreamed of their lovemaking it was with her own Gray as he had been, not as he was now. She had not once dreamed of his coming back, and now she wondered if it was because she knew, in spite of all her brave resolution to hang on, that it would not be the same man who returned to her.

# Chapter 15

The house felt different, and it was good to be home. When she'd left it two weeks ago, she hadn't been able to contemplate a life ahead without Gray; now she could, not joyously, but with some confidence that she and the boys would manage if they had to. Whatever Gray was doing now, she didn't know, and nobody else did either, so she wouldn't be informed.

In just a week the garden had grown even more promising, and she had a half dozen healthy tomato plants to set out. Though Peter and Chris spoke longingly of their frog and foal friends on the farm, they were happy to be back with their trucks and boats and their cove with its tide pools. Kevin had put out the haul-off for the dory, and she floated off there in all her blazing blueness.

"Tomorrow we'll go fishing," she promised the boys. "Tonight we'll take it easy and get a good sleep. Besides, the tide's wrong." Peter had already learned that one couldn't argue with the tide.

Kevin came around at twilight to bring the key he'd used. He welcomed her back with a bag of cherries and new fishlines for her and the boys. He thanked her for his graduation gift.

"I thought they'd go on your desk at college and remind you of home," she said.

"I'll always keep them, wherever I go," he said. He refused any pay for house-sitting. "I enjoyed it. It was great being here alone at night, having the TV to myself, reading as late as I wanted to. Every night I'd go down to the wharf before I went to bed and just look and listen. I'm beginning to think I was meant to be a hermit."

"How will you stand it in college next fall?"

He grinned. "I'm trying hard not to think about it."

"Listen, did anybody try anything? I was a little worried about Graduation Night, in case you stayed away till dawn."

"Heck, I was back here by midnight. That all-night bash is fine if you've got a girl, but nobody wants any unattached males roving around."

"Wasn't there some unattached girl you could have dated? Don't answer that, it's none of my business."

"My mother asked me the same thing. Says if I gave anybody else half a chance, I'd get over Dorri. Well, I guess I *am* over it. I mean, I'm facing facts. But I don't want anybody else for a good long while." His eyes watered and he grumbled, "Darn allergy."

He's such a darling, she thought, and he'd hate me if he knew I called him that. "You've got plenty of time," she said. "College is a whole new world. It's like being born again."

"I wouldn't mind a new incarnation. I can think of a lot of improvements to make on the new model."

She walked out to the car with him. The white-throats

were singing in the dusk; the air smelled of blossoming apple trees and lilacs, seasoned with salt tide. "It was probably a good thing I did get back here that night," he said suddenly. "They picked up Damon and Parris Cade over in Harper's Cove around one in the morning trying to rip off an outboard motor. Mac's dog barked and got him up, and he turned a spotlight on them, too late for 'em to get their ski masks on. But Damon went for his pistol." He chuckled. "Fastest gun in the East he's not. Got it all fouled up in his belt and almost shot a toe off. Anyway, Mac and his wife made a positive identification. And the Amity police were waiting for them on their own dock. They had some other stuff they'd picked up earlier. It's all in your *Patriot* there." He nodded at the mail on the washer.

"Thanks. I'll read all about it. What do you think will happen to them?"

"Slap on the wrist, suspended sentence." He shrugged. "I figure it's just a question of time before they do something really bad, or somebody wipes one of them out."

"You think they might have stopped off here if you hadn't been here?"

"It's a possibility," he said somberly. He got into the car.

"Look," she said, "I know you'll be busy now with your job, but if you could just help me get that skiff down, that's all I'd ask. Could you come around some evening?"

"Tomorrow, right after work. How's that?"

"I'll appreciate it."

Her sleep that night was light, excited, *fast*, as if she had fever. The bed felt too warm. She kept thinking how lucky she was not to be depressed, then wondered why, but not too hard; she was like someone awaiting an amputation and sedated with what the medical profession called a mood-elevator.

In the morning she and the boys went down to the cove to dig clams for bait. Then they went back to the house to have a mug-up and wait for the tide to rise a little higher. The boys were enchanted with their new lines, the bright-green twine wound on yellow plastic reels, the little leads, the shiny hooks. She didn't expect to do much fishing herself, what with keeping the boys from hooking themselves or each other, but that would certainly occupy her mind to the exclusion of almost everything else.

She was making some sandwiches for them to have for lunch aboard the dory, a great thing for the children even if they were only twenty-five feet from shore, when Carrie Sears came.

She was instantly on guard, not so much against Carrie as to protect her new insulation. She hoped that if she kept the boys in the kitchen Carrie wouldn't say too much.

"*Good* morning, Carrie!" she said with a warning heartiness.

"I suppose it's good for somebody." There was a suggestion of a whine. "Not for Rupe and me, with that poor child so scared she won't even call for fear of somebody making trouble for her."

"Where is the poor child?" Astrid asked.

Carrie took off her dark glasses and gave her a cold, bulging stare. "Who knows? Haven't *you* heard?"

"Why should I hear anything? I'm the last person to be informed."

"And no wonder! You've driven them away, you know.

I saw the bruises on her throat. I know the threats you made."

"Be quiet, Carrie," said Astrid politely. "Have you boys tidied your room yet? You'd better do it now, or we won't go fishing."

"Oh, all right," Peter said in a martyred tone. "Come on, Chris." They went up the back stairs. Astrid shut the door behind them.

"Now, Carrie," she said, "what was I supposed to have done?"

"Tried to kill Dorri right there on Main Street in the face and eyes of everybody. Gray had to fight to protect her! Well! Do you think he's going to stay around here and let her be harmed? No, *ma'am!* When they came to the house that day, Dorri joked about you waiting for them with a machine gun, but she hugged and kissed Rupe and me so *hard*, I should have known *something* was going on." Carrie's voice thickened. She blew her nose. "And she hasn't called since! Over a week now!"

"Well, when she does call, you tell her they can have each other, with my blessing."

"If you'd only made your mind up earlier," Carrie said tearfully. "Now they may never come back."

"We can always hope, can't we?"

"And those poor little boys, deprived of their father—"

"You can't blame that on me, Carrie."

"If you'd acted halfway civilized," Carrie snapped, "they could be with him part of the time."

"Let's not talk about who's civilized and who isn't," said Astrid.

"What will you tell them about him?"

"That's my business, Carrie."

"You were always stuck-up! No wonder Gray was glad to get shed of you. The stuff that Dorri told me—"

"Goodbye, Carrie," said Astrid, opening the screen door for her. She was beginning to tremble again inwardly. Carrie left in noisy tears, but managed to shut them off when she got into the car.

Afterward Astrid wondered if Gray had come here from the Sears place to get some of his own clothes. She went up and looked in his chest of drawers and his closet and saw that many of his things were gone. It was really over, then. The amputation had already taken place. The legal divorce would be nothing but a technicality.

"Come on," she called to the boys. "Let's go fishing!" They actually got a few pollock.

Celia Whitehouse, Kevin's mother, called in late afternoon. She was brusque but not rude. "Kevin had to come home sick from the store today, Astrid. He's worried about something he was going to do for you tonight, so he made me call you."

"Oh, just get a skiff out, it's not important," Astrid assured her. "Tell him not to worry. What's the trouble?"

"Chills and fever, nausea, the back-door trot. Some bug going around, I suppose. What we used to call summer complaint."

"Well, I hope he gets over it quickly, and tell him to forget the skiff. Fletch or Cam will probably show up here any time and one of them will help me."

"Thanks," Celia said flatly. Astrid was left with the impression that Celia thought Kevin had done enough to salve his conscience and should now get on with his own business, a part of which should be a survey of available girls. Well, I don't blame her, Astrid thought. He should have a girl, or at least be in a group. Maybe she thinks he's getting a romantic crush on me. Which shows what's in store for me when Peter and Chris get up there.

Nora and Fletch came around that evening, but Fletch had a kink in his back, so she didn't ask him to help her. He didn't know how he'd gotten the kink; he woke up with it one morning and could hardly get out of bed. "Likely my reward for thinking harsh thoughts," he said with a wry little smile.

"Fletch, don't tell me you ever had harsh thoughts about anyone," Astrid said.

"I'm human," he said with unusual sharpness. "But I learned young about my temper, and it kind of scared me. So I've worked at keeping it in line ever since."

"What are you going to do about Gray?" Nora asked her.

"Start the divorce as soon as I know where he is," said Astrid. "For irreconcilable differences."

"What about custody of the boys?"

"I don't want to think about that," Astrid admitted. "I don't want Dorri to have anything to do with them, but I don't really want to cut them off from him. If he shows up, maybe we can work out something in time. But if he's left for good..." She shrugged. "They've really cast us off, I guess. Dorri's a telephone addict but she hasn't even called her mother, and I'm sure if she'd called one of her sidekicks like Mavis Carter, the news would be around by now."

"He sold his pick-up that day," Fletch said. "Cam saw it at Limerock Ford and went in and asked about it. He'd have taken his tools, of course. They've probably gone where he thinks he can find work." He opened his hands in a gesture of sad resignation. "Maybe as far as California, or even Alaska."

"Maybe I did drive them by not being cooperative," Astrid said uneasily.

"Don't talk so foolish!" Nora scolded her.

"You got a couple of aspirin?" Fletch asked her. "I dunno but what I might have to go to an osteopath. We're starting on a new house next week and here I am feeling like Father Time."

She got him the tablets. "And no more pay checks," she warned him. "We're on our own now. I'm going to find something to do when I get myself sorted out."

"You won't turn down anything we'd like to give the boys," Nora said.

"No, I'd appreciate that, but I refuse to become the family burden."

Cam and Harriet were on a short trip between jobs, so he couldn't help with the skiff, and Kevin's virus attack lasted for nearly a week. But there was a stretch of muggy, damp, foggy days, warm but too wet for work on the skiff even if they'd had her out. They hiked in the woods and around the shore and did errands in the car. She worked up more firewood. In the house she baked for the freezer and made herself some slacks and shorts. She had a great compulsion to pack every hour to overflowing, and when bedtime came she sank like a stone.

Every time the telephone rang she thought it was Gray, calling from a safe distance to ask her what she'd wanted of him that day, or Carrie to say Dorri had called. But if they were on the move all the time, and really afraid of being brought back by the law, that might muzzle her. It would probably be the first thing that had ever done so.

With the start of the weekend the good weather came back, the first summer people, and Kevin, late on Saturday afternoon. He was paler, skinnier, and seemed to have grown about six inches. "I guess I'm not contagious now," he said sheepishly.

"But are you weak?"

"Because we want to get the skiff down!" Peter danced around him. "I'm going to paint her all myself, and her name is *Ibex!* And I'll row you all around the cove, Kevin," he bragged.

"You'd better learn how first," said Kevin.

"I'll learn fast."

"I'll row too," Chris said.

"Not till you're four!" Peter cried jealously. "And then *I'm* going to have a dog, and I'm going to school too!"

"Don't feel too bad, old boy," Kevin said to Chris. "You'll get there." He looked at Astrid, blinking. "Wouldn't it be great to be that little again and starting in all new?"

"Dear Kevin, you aren't that *old*. And neither am I. We can always start in all over again."

"But not like that." He glanced down at the two heads crowding around his legs, then sighed heavily. "Well, let's get the skiff."

She took the key off its hook. "I haven't been near the place since I came back, haven't needed to."

The boys ran ahead of them down the slope, surefooted as young goats, shouting just for the joy of it. But at the fishhouse they became quiet, waiting in suspense while Astrid put the key in the padlock and turned it and the lock sprang open. Ardently they helped to shove back the sliding door and heaved themselves up over the high step. Imprisoned heat rushed out, scented in a way to stop Astrid on the threshold. She and Kevin looked at each other.

"Good Lord, something's gotten in here or underneath and passed on," she said, euphemistically for Peter's benefit. He was already halfway up the loft stairs, saying, "Pee-*ew*, something stinks!" He and Chris breathed deeply and with enthusiasm. Kevin took two long strides across the room and picked them off the stairs, swung around and deposited them outside.

"Stay right there, men," he ordered. "Just in case it might be—uh—feline," he said to Astrid. "I'll go look." He went on up to the loft."

"Don't go out on the wharf, sit on the doorstep," she said to the boys. They obeyed. She looked down at them in the sun-filled doorway, yellow head and dark, small shoulders under striped jerseys, hands on bare knees.

"Hey, look at the loon, Chris," Peter instructed. Chris was brightly obedient. It was a sheldrake, but that didn't matter.

"Oh God," Kevin mumbled up in the loft. "Dear Jesus, no."

"What are you praying about up there?" she called. She started up, but he cried out, "No, don't!"

He appeared at the head of the stairs, falling over something on the way, and braced himself with a hand against the slant of the roof. His face was contorted, and he made a little whimpering sound.

She said sharply, "Kevin, what *is* it?"

"Go away from here. Take the kids." He started down,

and she backed away to give him room. He was an ugly yellowish color. He jumped off the stairs before he reached the foot, and when the children looked around, he shouted at them, "Come on, men, let's split! Hornet's nest up there!"

He grabbed up a child in each arm and started for the house in his long-legged, seemingly effortless lope, the boys laughing and kicking. With fear and horror she watched them go. It hadn't been just for a dead cat, that whimper and that dirty color. She turned back into the fishhouse and went slowly up the steps to the loft.

They lay sprawled in the skiff, dropped there like dolls. Time and the heat up here under the roof had not been gracious.

# Chapter
# 16

**G**ray lay on his back, bent awkwardly over the middle seat. Dorri had been tumbled in on top of him, her round bottom in tight jeans canted toward the roof, her legs dangling over the gunnel. One bare foot pointed toward Astrid; pale greenish-gray, slightly mottled. Her long hair fell forward in a curtain past her face and over Gray's.

Astrid backed down one step at a time, afraid to take her eyes off the scene, but finally she was below the floor level. She went out and slid the door closed and walked up to the house. What she had seen had been so unreal, like a waxwork representation of some famous crime, that she could hardly believe she had seen it; her brain could have created it out of intolerable strain. But she knew her brain wasn't disordered. And Kevin had nearly fallen downstairs in his escape from the scene; he had grabbed the children and run, so he had seen it too.

In a way it was all very like her experience when Gray told her he was going away with Dorri. You knew it could not be so, but it *was* so, and you were not insane, only destroyed.

In the house the children were staring awestruck at the bathroom door. She could hear Kevin retching. Chris ran to her and she picked him up. He wrapped his arms tightly around her neck and silently clung. Peter hurried to her and hugged her legs. "Kevin's throwing up and throwing up," he said.

"Yes, he's been sick," she said. "He shouldn't have come out today." She caressed Peter's head. "Now let me telephone." She sat Chris on the washer, where he remained without moving, looking with solemn dark eyes at the bathroom door. Peter still hung onto her, the superiority of four quite forgotten. They sensed something; they were like animals hearing thunder long before the human ear picked up the slightest vibration.

She dialed Dinah, and Ben answered. She spoke with deliberation. "Ben, could you and Dinah do me a great favor and come and get the children right away? This minute? I'd like them out of the way for the night."

"Be right there," said Ben. Bless the non-askers of questions.

"How'd you like to spend the night with Joanie and John?" she asked the boys. Peter began to brighten; Chris's lower lip expressed doubt. Panic needled her stomach. "How'd you like to shake hands with Poochie?" she asked with desperate gaiety. Chris smiled and started to wriggle off the washer. She caught him. "Let's get your pajamas and things, then."

"I'm going to teach Poochie a new trick," Peter announced. "When I think up one."

When they came down the back stairs, Kevin was out

of the bathroom, not quite so white but still looking bad. His head was wet from a dousing. "I'm sorry," he muttered.

"Why? You've still got a touch of summer complaint," she said briskly. The skiff kept flashing before her eyes, and that foot, a slide returned again and again by a mad projector. "You got up too soon."

"At least I can make some telephone calls for you."

"Not till Ben comes for the kids."

"You want some tea or something?" His teeth were chattering.

"You could use it," she said. "Yes, put the kettle on."

"Let's go out and watch for Uncle Ben," Peter said to Chris, and they went out the back door. Kevin's shaking hands were having a hard time with the teakettle, and she took it from him, half filled it, and put it on the stove. Then she got a down jacket from a hook in the cellarway and said, "Put this on."

He wouldn't touch it. "It's his, isn't it?" He looked sick again. She glanced at the jacket and thought, Gray will never see another winter. The jacket dropped from her hand, which had opened by itself as if all the nerves in it had just been severed. As if the hand had been cut off.

Ben and Dinah drove in, with their children in the back seat. Poochie's head hung panting out the window. She put Chris and Peter into the car, and rapturous giggles and shrieks resounded as Poochie greeted them. Ben and Dinah followed her into the house, and when she started to tell them, Kevin headed for the bathroom again. She found her mouth and tongue weren't working well, but she managed to speak.

"They're dead. We just found them in the skiff in the

fishhouse loft. I don't know how they—just that they're dead." Dinah, white-faced and silent, reached for her, but she moved away and turned off the heat under the teakettle.

"Do you want me to call the police?" Ben asked, stolid as granite and as gray.

"Yes, please. I was going to, but I don't know how well I'll do."

He went to the telephone, and Astrid walked quickly across the hall to the living room. Dinah followed her. "Listen, I'll keep the children as long as you want."

Astrid could hear Ben's leisurely low voice in the kitchen, but not the words. Not that she needed to hear the words. It had happened. *It had happened.* It was Gray she had seen in the skiff.

"Thanks, Dinah," she said above a roar like surf in her ears. She sat down on the sofa and put her head to her knees until the roaring subsided.

"I'll stay with you," Dinah was saying from up near the ceiling somewhere. "Ben can take the boys back."

"No need. Just keep the boys busy. They know something's very wrong."

Ben appeared in the doorway. "I called Cam too, and he'll get Fletch. That all right?"

"Oh yes, thank you, Ben. I didn't know how to tell them."

He cleared his throat and said, "What about calling Dr. Morey? You might need something."

"Like what?" Her voice cracked. "Nobody can supply what I need."

Dinah's face began to break into odd planes; tears ran

over her freckled cheeks. She tried to embrace Astrid, who said, "Don't, or I'll dissolve altogether. Just take care of the boys."

"Come on, Dine," Ben said. "Let's get them away before the cruiser comes."

If she had thought before this that the evenings were long, she knew now how short they had really been. The first trooper came, and he called George Rollins to take over traffic duty on the main road; the trouble with these scanners that everybody had nowadays, he said, was that not only the crooks knew where the police were, but the ordinary citizen knew where disaster had hit and rushed to the spot. Here, the immediate townspeople were more likely to stay out of the way, unless they could help the family somehow, but youngsters roving around in search of excitement would collect. The trooper explained this to Kevin, who sat huddled in the rocking chair trying to drink scalding tea, his eyes shiny and opaque as marbles, and to Astrid, who nodded politely at intervals as if it were a social occasion; all the time that full-color slide of the skiff in the loft kept coming back.

Cam, Fletch, and Nora arrived together, and while she tried to tell them about it, the cars from the Bureau of Criminal Investigation came, the medical examiner, and the ambulance. The activities at the fishhouse seemed to go on for hours while the family sat in the kitchen, stunned into silence. Astrid had wanted to send Kevin home, but the first trooper said he must stay until they'd taken down his story.

"But he's sick," she argued. "He should be in bed."

"Can't we make him comfortable?" Nora asked, glad to have something to do. "Come on, Kevin, we'll tuck you up on the sofa. How about some blankets, Astrid?"

"There's a steamer rug." Kevin went with them, blushing, miserable both with his stomach and his embarrassment. When they had left him and came back to the kitchen, Cam was pacing, and Fletch sat at the table with his head in his hands; Astrid wondered if he were praying for Gray's soul, which had escaped him while his back was turned.

"Oh, my God, the Searses!" The words erupted as soon as she thought them. She looked around wildly at the telephone, but Cam stopped his pacing and put an arm around her and led her to the rocker.

"Harriet's gone over there," he said gently. "She's about the only close relative Carrie has around here, so she went."

"Oh, thanks, Cam. But what are they doing down there that takes so long?" She didn't hear his answer, because of the intolerable, unacceptable pictures of Gray being bundled around like a life-sized doll. Ken and Barbie Doll. What if they were really mannequins down there, and it was all some immense, complicated, practical joke Dorri had dreamed up and managed to pull off? Figures from a department-store window? She knew somebody who'd got them for her. After all, Astrid hadn't seen their faces. Any minute now the lieutenant in charge would come in, contemptuous and scowling. "I don't know what's going on around here, but—"

It was all so clear that for an instant she wanted to tell the others it was all a bad dream from which they were about to waken. Then in the next instant she knew it was no dream, just as she had known who it was in the skiff, faces or not; just as she had been rocked backward by the smell.

At last the ambulance left, and all the cars but the first cruiser and one of the Bureau cars. The trooper came into the house with a big youngish man in a dark gray suit, incongruously well groomed, even elegant by contrast with this roomful of worn-out and rumpled people.

"I'm Lieutenant Hobart," he said, low-keyed. He had black hair and extremely blue eyes, rugged features that called for burly seafaring sweaters rather than charcoal urbanity.

"How do you do?" Astrid heard herself saying, as if it were a social gathering. "I'm Astrid Price." She introduced the family. Nora said "Hello," the men nodded stiffly.

"You can pick up the personal effects at the hospital tomorrow," he said. "Now I have a few questions to ask, if you don't mind."

Lightheadedly Astrid wondered if the blue tie had been picked out by some woman to match his eyes, or if he were vain enough to choose for himself. She was ashamed of her frivolity, but she was feeling a little drunk.

"First, can I ask you a question?" Cam's voice was rough and defiant; it had to be, to get out the next words. "How did they die?"

"They were shot," said Hobart, still low-keyed. I suppose they're trained to that, Astrid thought. He was folding back the cover of a small notebook. "There'll be autopsies, of course, and I can't tell you anything more right now."

"Shot *there* in the building?" Cam persisted.

"We think they were brought there dead. Mrs. Price, when did you last see your husband? I understand you two were separated." Who'd told him that?

"Yes, we were." Oddly enough his manner made the answering fairly simple, since he wanted only concrete facts. "I saw him about three weeks ago." She checked by the calendar. "On a Monday." Main Street, and the girl's pulse beating wildly under her thumb. "I went away the next day, Tuesday. I was up in Parmenter for two weeks, until last Tuesday."

"And you haven't been in your building down there since you came back?"

"There was no need to. I was busy with other things. Then we went to get the ski—sk—" She got all tangled up with the hideous word. He nodded and turned to Kevin.

"What's your connection here? Are you a relative?"

"No, sir. I do heavy chores, and I slept in the house while Astrid was away." He had gotten hold of himself now; he was composed and manly. "I came over this afternoon to get the skiff down for her."

"You slept at the house for how long?"

"Two weeks."

"Then nobody was around here during the days for that period?" He looked from Kevin to Astrid.

"There should only have been George Rollins, to check, and the CMP man to read the meter," Astrid answered. "I was here one day. That would be a week ago last Monday, Graduation Day. I did a washing, attended to my mail, and so forth."

He went back to Kevin. "In all that time, did you ever notice anything at night, hear anything out of the ordinary?"

Kevin bristled. "You think if I *did* I'd have pulled a pillow over my head and hoped it would go away?"

"You might have been waked up by some sound," the lieutenant explained, "and then not heard anything more. Sometimes that happens, and afterwards you think the sound was part of a dream."

"Well, that didn't happen to me," said Kevin belligerently. Color came into his face. "Taking care of somebody's house, I'd have investigated anything strange, even if it turned out to be nothing but a dream. I'll tell you what *did* happen, though!" He hauled his breath in sharply and appealed to Astrid. "I never told you, Astrid, because I thought it was over and done with, and I didn't want you to be scared, you've got enough to worry you."

Now what? she thought drearily. Fletch, silent this long, said her words aloud, patient and grieving. "Now what?"

"Graduation Night, when I drove in around midnight, somebody'd been in the house. The back door was standing open. I thought maybe you'd come back, or even Gr—" He gulped audibly. "But there wasn't any car. And when I went in, nobody was here. Some chairs were knocked over, and the drawers of the desk pulled out, but that was the only thing I could see out of place through the whole house. And I know I locked it in the morning."

"You didn't call the police or the constable?" Hobart asked.

"What good would it do? I could damn well figure who it was, but I couldn't prove it, and if they got hauled in for questioning on my say-so, they'd have come around here the next night and really wrecked the place, and me too." He was warming up with righteous indignation.

"Listen, that bunch have started carrying guns too. Just ask *him*."

The officer glanced at the trooper, who nodded. "Yes, handguns and ski masks. We picked them up about two the next morning for attempted burglary not far from here."

"Two coves away," Kevin said excitedly.

"All right." The lieutenant quieted him. "Now, just how thorough were you in your inspection of the premises?"

"Well, I looked in all the upstairs rooms. First I brought in a baseball bat I had in my car, just in case somebody was still here. Then I checked the keys, to see if they'd gotten into the barn or in the fishhouse." Another loud gulp. "That one *was* gone. So I went down there." He laced his big hands together and the knuckles cracked. "The padlock was open, hanging in the door with the key in it. I looked inside and all the tools were on the bench, as far as I could see, so I figured something had scared them off. If they came by boat, they probably heard my car coming. She's plenty noisy. I just snapped the padlock and brought the key back to the house. I'm *sorry*, Astrid," he said imploringly.

"Why? You were only trying to spare me."

"Everybody's been saying nothing will happen to that bunch until they commit murder!" Nora exclaimed. "And now they've done it!"

Fletch put his hand over hers. His face was austerely calm.

"Gray must have walked in on them," Cam said softly. "Nobody saw him after that day. But what in hell did they do with his car? Didn't you see that anywhere, Kevin?"

Kevin said blankly, "No."

"It's probably in one of the Limerock quarries," Cam said. "*Jesus.*"

"Cam," Fletch murmured.

"I'm praying, brother," Cam said ferociously. "Can't you tell?"

Hobart murmured something to the trooper, who went out. Then he turned pleasantly to Astrid. "By the way, Mrs. Price, did you try to get in touch with your husband that day you were here?"

She felt as blank as Kevin had been a moment ago. Her mind moved slowly, obscured by wreathing fogs. Finally she said, "Yes, I went to Partridge Point and left a note for him. But he never called."

The officer said, "I wondered." He took an envelope from inside his coat. "This was in the girl's hip pocket."

*She hid it! He never knew!* She thought she shouted it, but everyone looked the same, so they hadn't heard. "Yes, that's my note," she said numbly.

# Chapter 17

The trooper brought in another man, also in plainclothes, introduced as a Sergeant Something-or-other; by this time Astrid felt incapable of assimilating any more information. Impersonally polite, he took their fingerprints. "For purposes of elimination," Hobart explained. "Your prints should be around the place. We're looking for the foreign element, you might say. I hope you haven't polished everything too thoroughly, Mrs. Price." His manner was quite pleasant.

"Don't worry. I'm not that much of a housekeeper," she answered.

"What can you expect to find after all this time?" Cam asked. *Blood?* Astrid wondered giddily. Ridiculous. Everything was achingly bright, clean, and familiar.

"I'm not sure," he answered candidly, "but we can hope."

"Then let's hope some Cade prints are left and in perfect condition," Nora said. "If they get away with this, I may go after them myself."

While the rooms were dusted for prints, the family sat at the table, glazed with fatigue, arguing feebly. Nobody wanted to leave Astrid at the house, and she refused to go away from it and didn't want anybody to stay. They had to shift chairs occasionally so the sergeant could go on with his work. Hobart, coming back into the kitchen, said, "If you're worried about her safety, the sheriff's department will be keeping an eye on the place."

"Thank you," she said with genuine gratitude for his ending the argument. "And I have just remembered, some neighbors were here earlier to take the boys, their prints should be here too. Ben and Dinah Morison."

"Thank you." He made a note. Eventually their work was done.

When the cars had gone away, nobody spoke at once. Then Fletch sighed heavily and got out of his chair as if he felt very old.

"I'd better find out where Harriet is," Cam said. "If she's stuck over at the Searses with the two of them gone off their heads, I'll have to get her out of there quick. Mind if I call home, Astrid?"

Harriet was home and was telling Cam her experience when another car drove in. Fletch went out to the door; those inside heard Carrie Sears's shrill cries. "Where's my baby? We've been all over Limerock, nobody would tell us anything!" She pushed past Fletch into the kitchen.

"They're probably at the hospital, Carrie," Fletch said.

Rupe's pinched, ghastly face almost smiled. "At the *hospital?* Then she's not dead—she's only hurt, is that it?"

Fletch put an arm about the other man's shoulders. "I'm sorry, Rupe. But they're both gone."

"What did you do to her?" Carrie screamed at Astrid. "She was afraid of you, and she was right! She showed me the marks!"

"Whatever happened," Fletch said, "it was when Astrid was away."

Carrie crumpled noisily against Rupe's chest. Over her head he asked patiently, "Can somebody tell me what happened?"

"It looks as if they came around here one night and surprised somebody in the house," Cam said.

"And all this time I thought she was safe in Texas or California," Rupe said in wonder. "And she was right here." He swayed slightly. Fletch steadied him. Nora removed Carrie from his chest and sat her firmly in a chair. "Oh God," Rupe said in a queer voice. "Oh God." He put his arm against the wall and his head against it and began to cry.

The Searses left soon, refusing Cam's offer to drive them home. Cam left after that. Fletch and Nora were reluctant but went at last. Astrid took a long hot bath and went upstairs, but now she couldn't go into her and Gray's bed, knowing that he would never come back to it. She stood on the threshold, wobbly with tiredness, thinking, Never again. Never. Never. Never. I'll chop it up and burn it.

She went across to the spare room. Kevin had left the bed freshly made up as he'd found it, and she crawled in with a heating pad to fight off the chills.

The instant she shut off the light, she was going up the loft steps again and seeing the foot, so she put on the light. It was day and the birds were singing before weariness at last swamped her, bad pictures and all, and she slept.

When she woke, the sun was shining in the room, and someone was hauling traps in the cove. She remembered at once what had happened. She lay there thinking, If

I'd gone down to the river that day and found them, this might never have happened. She couldn't think of any good reason to blame herself, other than masochism, but one always thinks, *If only* ... Dorri had seen the note first and hidden it; otherwise Gray would have called her. But how do you know, she relentlessly questioned herself, that they still wouldn't have come over here that night and run into those vicious kids? They were going away and it probably wasn't an instant decision; if he'd called, he'd have told you on the telephone that they were going and that you could divorce him for desertion if you wanted, but he was on his way. And he wouldn't have come for his clothes until he knew you were out of the house.

So they went somewhere, probably drove some distance to eat, to use up the time between their stop at Carrie's and their visit here, so as to be sure not to meet you; maybe he knew about the note after all and decided to ignore it, not wanting an argument. Or, if he *didn't* know, Dorri certainly did, and managed to keep him from meeting you. But why, if I sounded willing to talk divorce? Why didn't she want to have the satisfaction of hearing me say it, so she could laugh in my face?

It was so clear a vision that it was an acute shock to realize that Dorri had been reduced to a limp long-legged doll dropped and broken by a giant child.

And so had Gray. She was glad she hadn't been able to see his face; it was Cam who'd made the formal identification.

What you want, she told herself wearily, is something else to remember beside that skiff and the way he looked up in Williston after you slapped Dorri's face. You want to remember that you talked together at last as two reasonable people who'd been happily (at least on your side) married for six years. You want to remember seeing in his eyes the recognition of you as someone he had loved and maybe still did in spite of this insanity.

She cried then, cried and cried, and fell asleep again.

She woke around noon, as lame all over as if she'd lain stiffly on a board for hours. That reminded her of morgues and autopsies. She went downstairs and washed in cold water to wake herself up, made strong coffee, and called Dinah.

"The boys are fine," Dinah said. "They went to Sunday school this morning, and now all four and the dog are digging clams. We'll keep them as long as you want."

"Would you bring them back this afternoon? I need them."

"Sure you do." Dinah was subdued. "Listen, it was on the news this morning, but no real information." She cleared her throat. "What do they think happened?"

"They were shot, Dine," she said. "The police are investigating a lead. You'll hear it soon enough."

"When's the—uh . . ." Again Dinah was unable to use the proper word.

"We don't know. They're doing autopsies."

"I just can't believe this is happening!"

"Neither can I. I'll see you later, Dine."

She was shaky and drank more coffee before she called Nora to tell her she was all right and had had some sleep. "How's Fletch?"

"He never slept, neither did I. It's a good thing it's not a work day. He and Cam are a pair this morning. One of them would be sure to saw off a finger or fall off a ladder.

And you poor thing! It's been rotten for you for so long, and now this."

"I have the boys to keep me busy, and you concentrate on Fletch. Goodbye for now." She drank again; she could swallow liquid, but nothing solid. She thought of the way Gray used to calm her when she panicked, and then he himself had dealt her the most terrible blows, which she had had to bear alone.

The hardest thing to bear was the knowledge that the boys would forget him. They would forget the smell of his clothes, the scent of his skin, the sound of his voice, the feel of his arms when he lifted them, his laughter, the occasional spankings and scoldings, the promises, the joking, the good-night kisses. It was still fresh and alive and real to them now, but in a few years it would be gone. At times they would feel cheated to be without a father, but it wouldn't be Gray they felt cheated of, but an idea—at most a dream figure created from wishful thinking. And it wasn't the faceless hoodlums who had done this to her boys, but Gray himself.

There was so much to do, but here she sat, not having the energy to begin. Probably her mother should be notified, but that meant her arrival in a furor, and explanations that could never be left bleakly simple but must be taken to bits and analyzed to the last shred. And then she would say, We told you at the time you shouldn't marry him. . . . At the time she had objected to Gray only because he wasn't her choice; he'd been all right for young summer romance, but they'd expected a great deal more for Astrid, considering the life they lived. They'd given up gracefully. Liking Gray personally, her father died knowing she was happy. Since his death her mother had been on the wing, but in Astrid's letters and telephone talks she had always stressed her happiness.

If she could just wait until it was all over and then tell her mother that Gray had died suddenly—

*Gray had died suddenly.* No. She wouldn't have it, she couldn't bear it. All the time when she thought he had gone somewhere far away, and she had seen for the first time a possibility of being both free and whole, he had been lying there in the skiff under the roof, with Dorri's hair falling over his face.

She ran outdoors then to try to breathe.

Dinah brought the boys back and a basket of food all cooked. "I know you won't feel like cooking, but you've got to eat. You boys be sure to come see Poochie again. He really likes you. . . . Ben and I will do anything we can, Astrid. Just tell us."

Several people called to say the same thing, including the minister. She was grateful for the quiet kindnesses.

Kevin's mother phoned, not to offer concern. "I thought I'd speak to you while Kevin's asleep and couldn't hear."

"How is he, Celia?"

"He's not *good*. His father finally went against all our principles and made him drink a stiff toddy, to try to get him to sleep. I'm not letting him come over there any more, Astrid."

"I don't blame you." She began to feel exhausted again.

"He was so wild about that girl, he was nearly out of his mind when she did what she did. It seemed to take his mind up, hanging around doing chores for you, so we didn't object. Now I wish we had."

"I wish you had too. But I asked him how you felt about

it, Celia. I wanted to be sure." Oh, stop gabbling.

"It's not your fault."

But you think it is, because I'm Gray's wife. You're always to blame if you're a victim, just for being there.

"I know this is terrible for you, and I'm sorry," Celia said, "but we have to think of our child, the same as you have to think of yours."

"I understand."

"We're thinking of sending him to my brother in Connecticut until it's time for him to start college. He'll make a big fuss, but his father's still the boss."

"Good," said Astrid. "Goodbye, Celia."

"He could have been killed himself by those bums. We should bring back the death penalty."

"Yes. Goodbye," she said again and hung up. I think she hates me, she thought, because she can't hate Dorri any more.

She packed a supper and took the children down through the meadow to the shore so they wouldn't have to go anywhere near the fishhouse. They went out on a point where the deep combers rolled in from open sea and rattled the beach stones. Driftwood had been tossed high among the stunted spruces, and clean shells littered the short turf. They found a spray of ripe wild strawberries in a pocket where spray flew over them. Eider ducks and ducklings rode the offshore swells.

They stayed until nearly sunset. She cringed from the return to the house, to all that lay ahead. But the point would still be there and the good wildness of it. When this next week was over with, they could come back here and spend a whole day. Maybe in this place she would be able to tell the boys that Gray was dead.

George Rollins was looking at the garden when they got home. She'd carried Chris piggyback for the last half of the walk, but now a budding sense of male pride made him insist on being put down, tired as he was.

"Nice garden," George said. "What did you plant for beans this year?" They discussed gardens; he was trying new variations of tomatoes and corn.

"Will *you* help us get my skiff out?" Peter asked him. "Kevin was going to, but then he got sick."

"Don't you remember the hornet's nest?" Astrid said. "We have to keep it all shut up tight until they're gone."

"I remember," Peter said grumpily. "After that, will you help us, Mr. Rollins?"

"I sure will."

"Boys, carry what you can to the house and I'll be right along," she told them. She helped them load up again with the treasures they'd been lugging home and started them off.

"There'll be a skiff," she said to George, "but not that one. You didn't come by just to talk farming, George."

"Well, I thought you'd like to know they've taken in Damon and Parris Cade for questioning. Most of the Cade prints are already on record, and there were a couple of good sharp matching specimens somewhere in your house."

She shut her eyes, for a moment unable to breathe or to see but only to think, Those little monsters! George was saying in alarm, "You all *right?*" He had her by the elbow.

"I'm all right." She opened her eyes and the sunset brilliance blazed into them. "Go on."

"Well, they were out on bail till the Harper's Cove business comes up, but the police took the old man by surprise with a search warrant. Kids got all kinds of handguns and no permits for any of them. Oh, the pistol they had that night, the police already had that, and they've been having tests run and proved it was the one fired through some windows in various places, and so forth. So they've got them on several counts. Now they're having new tests done because of this."

"You mean," she said steadily, "that because of the autopsies the police have the bullets?"

"Yes. Little bastards. They've hanged themselves now, or would have, if we still had hanging in the state. Ought to bring it back."

They walked slowly up toward the house. The boys had gotten second wind and were rolling down the slope. "Cades are squealing their heads off now," George said harshly. "Scared foolish. Damon nearly went up the wall when they picked him up. They've had to have a doctor come to the jail and give him a shot. Parris just sits and stares. Says they were there but never saw anybody. And of course the old man's going to sue everybody."

He talked with the boys a few minutes, gave Astrid a box of fresh cookies his wife had sent to the children, and left. As if in a dream she got the boys ready for bed. So this was how it all finished. The great madness, the obsessions, the pain, the fury, all ended in an instant by a gun in a panicky hoodlum's hand.

That night she wrote her mother, setting out the facts in dry, lifeless sentences. "Please don't come until after it's over," she wrote. "I will need you more then. It's all confusion now."

# Chapter
## 18

**M**onday morning she had a call from someone, not Lieutenant Hobart, telling her that the autopsy reports were in, and the bodies were to be released. *The bodies*. Gray Price, that was, and Dorri laughing and tossing back her hair as she ran out to the waiting car. Not dust to be poetic about, but something to be disposed of as decently soon as possible. NO LITTERING. KEEP MAINE CLEAN.

She called Fletch, and he and Nora, Cam and Harriet came around to the house. School was out, and they brought along Fletch's oldest, Hugh, to stay with the boys. The day was gray; the new summer greens were seen through a blur of showers. The children could play indoors, and Hugh, a good mixture of his parents, could be trusted to be a referee and also field any awkward questions.

The thought of a funeral dominated Astrid's thinking with fresh horror, and she was relieved to find out that the rest of the family would agree to a simple graveside service. She hadn't believed that Fletch would consent;

but he was a realist along with everything else and knew that any minister who knew the situation would have a hard time talking about Gray at a formal service. He did ask Astrid if she minded if his pastor attended them at the grave, and she did not. After all, she and Gray had hardly ever gone to church here in town where the children went to Sunday school.

So the arrangements were made. They didn't see Gray. They returned to the house to have lunch together; they were hungry without appetite, as if the whole appalling affair had drained away even their physical substance. The other two women had brought hearty casseroles, fresh rolls, two rhubarb pies. Some neighbors had come while the family was away, and there was more food ranged on the dresser, including roast chicken and meat pies. "It's happening over our way too," said Nora. "None of us will have to cook for a week."

After lunch—which to Peter and Chris was an exciting occasion, like their Sunday dinners at their uncles' houses —the women wrapped much of the food for the freezer. When they left, Nora ordered Astrid to take a nap while the boys slept. "And if you can't sleep, you're going to see Ed Morey and have him give you something."

"I'll sleep," Astrid promised her, knowing she wouldn't; Nora knew that too.

She lay on the living-room sofa, but that was where Gray had slept those nights, or rather had lain awake trying to think what to say to her. She built a fire in the fireplace and sat on the floor with her back against a chair, watching the flames and hypnotized into a numbed, dreamy objectiveness.

Gray said he'd broken off whatever there'd been with

Dorri—a flirtation, a momentary surrender to temptation, a tightrope walk along the edge of—*what?* Foolishness, a disgraceful weakness, recklessness, even daring, but certainly nothing ever seen as danger. But Dorri, probably all meek tears and promises one night, hadn't been about to give up her older and married man. She'd bragged about him too much. Had she pulled the suicide threat on him from that motel where she'd called? Who'd driven her there in the first place and might have been listening with admiration to her telephone performance? Mavis Carter, probably.

Maybe we'll get lucky and *she'll* be found dead in a ditch, Astrid thought dispassionately. Girls like her and Dorri were vandals like the Cade boys.

Dinah came over, alone, and they sat quietly through the showery afternoon, drinking tea and keeping the fire going. She had been at a church fair in Amity and brought the boys presents—a large stuffed yellow-and-green frog for Peter and a brown owl for Chris. The boys were enchanted, and Peter at once composed an appropriate drama.

"It's a good thing it's an owl instead of a crow," Astrid said wryly. "I suppose owls eat frogs too, but it's a crow in the song."

"You mean the song about the frog who wanted to be a dancer in yellow? Peter was singing it to the kids the other night."

"Thank goodness he's been too busy to think of it around here. I don't think I could stand to sing it."

"Astrid, it's too soon to say this—"

"But you'll say it anyway."

"Yup! You're young, and someday you'll get over this, that's all I was going to say. You'll never forget it, but you'll get over it. I'm only saying this to brace myself up, because if anything happened to Ben I'd die. And if anyone told me I'd get over it, I'd belt 'em."

Astrid had to smile, which she hadn't believed possible.

Around supper time Dr. Morey stopped at the house without her having asked him; she suspected Nora. He was on his way home from delivering a baby at Limerock Hospital. "Have you got any more in your car?" Peter asked excitedly. "Can we go see?"

"Nope, that was the last one for the day," he said. He had brought Astrid a mild tranquilizer. "It won't make you dependent if you follow instructions. It won't dope you so you can't hear the kids, and you won't have a hangover in the morning. But you'll get some rest and be a lot more good to your children and yourself. You're a walking danger now."

It wasn't hard to give in, she was so tired. But she thought of something she needed urgently to ask him. It took courage because she didn't really want to know, but she *had* to know.

"You were at the hospital," she said diffidently. "Maybe you heard about the autopsies, or are they always kept a deep secret?"

"You mean nobody's told you yet?" He was mildly surprised. "Well, they haven't got around to it yet. Yes, I know. I don't think I'll get into trouble for telling you."

"I won't tell anyone that I've heard. Please."

The boys were oblivious, making loud engine noises. They were using a braided rug as an island to run their boats around. The frog and the owl were enthroned in the center of it.

"Well," he said reluctantly, "the girl was shot at fairly

close range in the middle of the forehead. The man was shot approximately here—" he tapped his own forehead at the hairline—"in what's called the superior sagittal sinus. The same weapon was used. The official reports will be a lot more technical and complicated."

"Something so little can do so much," she whispered. They watched the children for a few moments, then he got up to go. She went to the door with him.

"Thank you very much," she said formally. "For everything."

"Take it easy," he said. "Don't deny that anything's happened. Ride with it."

"I'm trying to."

He patted her shoulder. "Good girl." This made her want to burst into tears and bawl, square-mouthed, like the boys. But she didn't.

That night in the spare room she slept, waked, checked on the boys, and drifted to sleep again, oddly detached from events. However, she was alert in the morning, as he had promised. Nothing had grown any less painful with the passing of the night; in fact the agony seemed to be just getting into its stride, but because of the sleep she felt stronger.

Gray's service was to be that afternoon, and the children and Dinah's two would stay with Dinah's mother. Astrid planned to spend the morning mowing the lawn. She would not expect Kevin now; probably he had been already shipped out of town and was glad to go.

Waiting for the dew to dry somewhat before she started to mow, she was caught by the telephone and expected it to be one of the family to see how she was. It was Carrie Sears. Carrie's voice sounded thick, as if she were permanently stuffed up from weeping, but it was even more clangingly aggressive than before.

"I see by the papers you're having private services in the cemetery," she began. "Well, *we've* no reason to hurry *our* loved one into the ground. We're having a lovely service at the funeral home tomorrow."

Astrid flinched in actual pain. "Carrie," she said softly, "I'm so sorry for you and Rupe."

"She didn't get her big wedding, but she's getting a big ceremony now, and she'll be dressed in white and wearing the ring he gave her. It's too bad you didn't find them earlier so we could have an open casket. She'd have looked beautiful."

I don't believe this, Astrid thought. I'm having a weird reaction to the tranquilizer; I'm dreaming awake.

"I've been trying to round up pallbearers. Rupe's no good at all at organizing. I tried to get Kevin, and would you believe it, his mother won't let him? Wouldn't even let me ask him myself, for Dorri's sake. That boy is so tied to his mother's apron strings it's a shame. God know what'll happen to him."

Astrid thought she made some faint sound, but she wasn't sure. "Well, I just wanted to tell you," Carrie ran on, "in case you weren't reading the papers these days and didn't see the notice. I thought you might want to send some flowers. It's at Herbert's Funeral Home."

This time she knew she didn't utter anything. Carrie said with growing frustration, "*I* shall put flowers on Gray's grave, white ones, in memory of Dorri."

"Carrie, you'd better stop," Astrid warned her. "We're both wretched, and this kind of talk doesn't help either of us."

"I'll bet *you* knew they were there all the time!" Carrie shouted viciously and slammed down her telephone. Astrid went out to mow and did all the lawns, front, back, and sides, without even feeling the weight of the machine or a strain in her hands and legs.

But at the end of the chore she was exhausted, and she'd also exhausted the virulence she felt toward Carrie Sears. She actually slept during the boys' early naptime.

Two of the Price sisters had arrived the night before, and a third one had come that morning. Her mother called, saying that only her strep throat was keeping her away, in spite of Astrid's request. The family, the closest friends of its various members, and the minister met in the little cemetery. It was reached by a narrow road cutting through someone's woodlot, and out-of-towners would have never guessed where that road led. The hometowners wouldn't intrude, but there were flowers from some of them. The funeral director had tactfully held back Carrie's all-white spray but told Fletch about it and asked what to do. Fletch told him to send it either to the hospital or a nursing home.

"If only she doesn't show up here," Nora whispered.

"She won't dare," Harriet whispered back, fiercely. "I told her if she wants *me* to show up tomorrow she'd better stay away from here. And she wants me; I'm all the family she's got."

"Poor Carrie," Astrid said, meaning it. "I've got all of you."

There was an enormous spray from her mother. But it was the little bouquet from Kevin that almost broke her down, like the doctor's encouraging words. The minister spoke tenderly and briefly of Gray as one they had all loved, and his prayer was neither sentimental nor long. For a moment, as he said for Gray the familiar benediction beginning "The Lord bless thee and keep thee," and ending "And give thee peace," Astrid felt a loosening in her breast, like release, as if some eerie spell had been broken, and wherever Gray was, the horror was past and he was secure.

But there was no time to give in to it. She'd have liked to go home, picking up the boys on the way, and be quiet and alone with them. But the family was to gather at Fletch's, and she hadn't the strength to make her wishes known; besides, it would have done her no good. She was surrounded by their anxious love, swept on by it as if by a tidal wave beginning its long journey toward land. The sisters and their husbands made much of her. She was beseeched to visit in Connecticut, in Massachusetts, in western Maine. She appreciated it all, and yet she thought, What do they *know?* What can they *do?*

They would all go back to their lives, sadly at first but soon becoming involved again. She was the one who was starting out all new. The one element in her life which hadn't changed was her children, but that too had its foreign, frightening side when she contemplated raising them to manhood all by herself. Thinking about it made her ache to be with them, to touch them and assure herself that they were still little more than babies.

Finally she found Fletch sitting alone in the back yard, somberly looking off across the fields and stroking the big cat lying on his thigh. She sat with him for a few minutes, trying to recapture from the summer evening that sense of release she'd felt during the benediction, but it was gone.

"Will you drive me home, Fletch?" she asked.

"Of course." He lifted the cat gently off his lap. They didn't even go in to tell the others, and they didn't talk all the way back. When it was almost time to pick up the boys she said in a hurry, "Fletch, I keep blaming myself."

"I keep blaming *my*self," he said mildly. "It's natural, I guess. But maybe I drove him away."

"He loved you, Fletch."

"He loved *you*."

"Stalemate," she said, and he half smiled.

When the boys were in bed, she wanted to call Kevin about the flowers, but she was afraid of being snubbed by his mother.

# Chapter 19

S he managed a fair night's sleep. Cam stopped in early on his way to the new job, to have a cup of coffee with her. She and Cam had always hit it off, even as youngsters, when Fletch was so serious and Gray, whom she'd adored from the start, was too shy.

"I hear the Cades are babbling from morning till night," he said. "They're even going back two or three years. Yes, they did this, they did that, sure they did, but never, *never*, did they ever shoot anybody. They're demanding lie-detector tests. And the old man's going to sue anybody he can for getting confessions under duress."

"What if it wasn't the Cades, Cam?" she asked.

"Of course it was! They probably didn't plan it, but they got caught fair and square, and they panicked. And they've been panicking ever since."

"But they stopped off at Harper's Cove to steal an outboard motor, and they still had the gun. That's not very sensible."

"Nobody ever said a Cade had to have brains. Just brass. Who the hell is *this?*" he snarled. A car was swinging in beside his truck. The boys, out early to play with their

cars in the sand pile, were as motionless and alert as squir-
rels. The men who got out called to them, and their wari-
ness broke up into smiles and answering shouts.

It was Lieutenant Hobart and Sergeant Something-or-
other, who went over to the sand pile and began talking
to the boys but were soon being talked at by Peter.

Astrid opened the door for Hobart. Her skin was lightly
prickling all over, except on her scalp, where it was drawing tight. In defense she looked to see if he wore a blue tie
this morning. It was paisley, which did absolutely nothing
for his eyes, she thought critically. She should tell him; if
he was really vain, it would be a mortal blow.

Mortal blow. Small bullet hole in the forehead and it
meant The End.

"Good morning," he was saying. For whom? For him?
He looked very healthy and cherished. She hoped for his
wife's sake that nobody ever put a bullet hole in *his* forehead.

First he told them how Gray and Dorri had died. She
pretended the doctor hadn't told her and suspected that
Cam was pretending too; the funeral director had probably
told him and Fletch.

"The car has been found," Hobart said. "It was run into
an old cutting in North Applecross woods. There's a poor
road through it, used mostly by hunters—"

"I know the place," Cam interrupted harshly. "Get on
with it."

"It was found by a couple of boys out for a hike. They
had the sense not to touch anything but came straight out
of the woods and called us. We now have the car. It had
been wiped clean of prints, but nothing seems to have been
stolen from it. Mr. Price's and the girl's bags were in the

car, his carpenter tools were in the trunk. The car hadn't been burgled, any more than the people had been robbed."

"What about her shoes?" Astrid was astonished by her own query.

His look was politely questioning.

"She was barefoot," she explained. That greenish bare foot pointing at her was going to be a very special kind of haunting for a long time.

"Oh yes. We looked for her shoes, I remember. There were several pairs, and sneakers, tossed into the car. She must have been going barefoot."

Astrid nodded seriously and then thought how ridiculously solemn they were, as if they'd settled some important diplomatic point. She wondered if she was going to crack up. But I *can't*, she thought, sitting up straighter and giving Hobart her most intense attention.

"Now there's something else I'd like to discuss," he said.

"Parris and Damon Cade were damn busy boys that night," Cam observed. "Walking all the way back from where they stashed the car."

"That's what I want to talk about," said Hobart. "According to the ballistics report, the weapon Damon Cade was carrying when he was arrested that night isn't the murder weapon, and nothing else in the family arsenal fits, either."

"How do you know they didn't have another one and drop it overboard somewhere?" Cam demanded. "They'd be damned fools to hang on to it. They knew enough to wipe their prints off the car, and I'm beginning to think the stop at Harper's Cove was some bollixed-up idea of camouflage. Like 'We're a couple of kids out stealing outboard motors, that's all!' Rotten little bastards! They probably dropped the gun overboard between this cove and Harper's."

"But if they went through all that," Astrid said slowly, "why didn't they stop to lock up the house and the fish-house?"

"Because Kevin drove in just as they got back from leaving the car! They were probably paddling out of the cove as fast as they could, not daring to start the motor, by the time he got into the house."

"It's all being taken into consideration," the officer said.

"Good God!" Cam exploded. "With all we've put up with from that bunch—with all the things they've done and been *caught* at—they've still kept free of the state prison. Those two are over eighteen by now, they can't be treated as juveniles any more, but they'll get away with this, wait and see! If they get jammed into a corner they'll trot out the baby and say *he* had the gun and didn't know it was loaded!"

"The Sheriff's Department is pretty happy with some of the information they've received from the boys," said Hobart. "I realize that's of no help to you. We're still not ruling the boys out, but we have to follow other lines of inquiry now."

"What could they possibly be?" Astrid asked. "Unless someone else tried to break in and Gr— and my husband surprised them."

"That's always possible. The Cade boys aren't the only ones, though sometimes it must seem that way." He sounded human. "The point is, there should have been a good deal of blood, at least from Mr. Price's wound. We didn't find it here, and we hoped to find it in the car, but we didn't. Mrs. Price, do you have a handgun?"

"No!" Cam said explosively.

"Yes," Astrid said at the same time.

Hobart lifted an eyebrow. "Who's right?"

Cam flushed. "What do you want to know for?"

"Someone could have found the gun and used it. Somewhere. What make is it, Mrs. Price? And will you get it for me?"

"I don't have one that I keep by me, not with two children running around. But there's a twenty-two-caliber revolver somewhere in this house. My husband never liked hunting, but we used to do target shooting."

"You sound as if you don't know where it is."

"I don't. Gray put it away somewhere so long ago, because of the children. I might have known once, but I don't remember."

"But you do know it's a twenty-two revolver."

"Ruger Bearcat, single-action. I remember because of the design on the cylinder. There's a bear and a mountain lion, and so forth."

"I remember that!" Cam exclaimed, not with any great satisfaction. "I thought he'd got rid of it years ago."

"No, he used to say that when the boys were old enough he'd teach them how to handle firearms, and that little gun was a real pet of his." She was surprised at being able to recollect and say these things. What would happen when the anesthesia wore off? There was a poem somewhere. . . . Her mind wandered off across far fields, searching.

Oh! dreadful is the check—intense the agony—
When the ear begins to hear, and the eye begins to see;
When the pulse begins to throb, the brain to think
    again—

Annoyingly a level voice prodded her. "What was that?" she asked, frowning.

"Would you see if you can find the revolver for us, Mrs. Price?"

"If someone's stolen it, it won't be here."

"But we won't know, will we, until you look?" He was sounding so very kind, as if he suspected her of going round the bend.

"I wouldn't know where to begin," she said. "There are so many nooks and crannies in this house."

"Would you object to professional help?"

"Not without a lawyer's advice first," Cam broke in. "Listen, Astrid, you can't just turn over your house like this; you've got rights you should protect."

"But the important thing is to find the gun," she said reasonably. "I'm not afraid of that, Cam."

"Then let the family do the searching. We'll all turn to, go right through from cellar to attic."

"I really think it would be better to let the police search, Cam," she said. "Then they'll be sure it's thorough."

He ran his hands crossly through his hair. "I've got to get to work, but damn it, I don't like this! If you don't look out for yourself, Astrid, somebody's got to! Will you call Todd Bingham, or Roscoe Searles, or anybody you want, and get some advice? And *follow* it?"

"Yes, I will, Cam," she said solemnly. She went to the door with him and kissed him on the cheek. "Thanks, and don't worry."

He looked aggressively past her at Hobart and tramped out. When she came back to the table the lieutenant said, "Will you call now?"

"No. I'll have to call eventually because of all the legal

things, but right now I'd only run for a lawyer if I had something to worry about."

"You're very composed, Mrs. Price."

"I haven't the strength to be anything else." Her voice shook on the last word. "Do you want to start searching now?"

"Not right this minute. Let's get back to your note, shall we?"

She sat down wearily opposite him. "That note," he went on, "is the only visible connection between those two and you for the whole period when you were away. We don't know that they came to the house on that day, but they were at the Sears house in the late afternoon, and her parents had the distinct impression they were coming here afterwards. But you say you didn't see them."

"No, and I stayed until half past four waiting for Gray to call." She found it incredible to be able to say his name, seeing him alive as she said it.

Studying his notebook, he said in a preoccupied way, like a doctor trying to ease his way toward telling the bad news, "We can't be sure that they were killed that night, but the last time they were seen or heard from was on that day, so it's all we have to go on. We could be wrong." He lifted his head and looked at her. "They could have died in daylight and the car hidden in the barn and disposed of any night in the last two weeks."

She was filling her lungs for breath with which to speak, though she didn't know what she'd say, when the telephone rang. She ran for it as for a life preserver. At the other end Kevin cleared his throat and said uncertainly, "Astrid?"

"Yes. *Yes.* Kevin, how are you?" She was actually

pleased. "I wanted to thank you for your flowers, but I didn't know if I should call."

"Yeah. Well. I kind of sneaked my order to the florist. It's not that my folks aren't sorry and all, but they're over-protective. I'm old enough to drink, vote, and fight a war, but they'll never admit it."

"That's parents for you," said Astrid, "and I speak as one. Wait until you're a father, Kevin. Anyway, thanks again."

She came away from the telephone and Hobart said musingly, "Kevin Whitehouse. We can't seem to get near that boy to go over his statement again. His mother insists he's sick."

"Well, he's had some kind of virus, I think. He came out too soon, and that night was no help. I wonder if they've checked him for mono." She could sympathize with Celia's desire to protect Kevin, even from her; she herself was afraid of becoming neurotically protective of Chris and Peter. She had to go now and look out at them. The sergeant was sitting on the chopping block smoking his pipe and being entertained.

"Did you think he might have left something out?" she asked Hobart. It helped to watch the dark and bright heads.

"Not on purpose. But he might have remembered something else by now. We'll see."

He went out to the car and called on the radio, then sat in the car writing something for a few minutes. She tried to fasten her mind down to hard detail. Where *would* the revolver be? Not in the steel strongbox, but she'd probably have to open that for them. Well, good luck to them, having to tackle the attic, which she'd been happily ignoring for months. By the time they went through her parents' trunks they'd know they'd been somewhere. And when they did turn it up from wherever Gray had hidden it, and it certainly hadn't been out of its hiding place for over two years, they would have to find another starting point.

It had all seemed so gruesomely easy when they thought that Dorri and Gray had surprised the Cades and been shot, carried to the fishhouse, and hidden away. It was easy until you wondered why they hadn't simply hurried for home the instant they were safe out of the cove in the dark, instead of stopping off at Harper's Cove for a spot of burglary.

Another unmarked car drove in with two men, and Hobart had a conference with them. This was all enthralling to the boys. Hobart brought the men in and introduced them; she didn't take in their names. She said, "There are only two locked containers in the house, the medicine cabinet and the strongbox. That's under the counter there." She brought the steel container out from the cupboard under the counter. "My key's in my handbag. I'll get it." Gray's key was on his key ring, but she couldn't make herself open the drawer where she'd put his things when Fletch brought them home from the hospital. She wondered dispassionately whether they would be looking for blood again.

Hobart had gone out and was standing by the sand pile listening to Peter explain his road system. "Well, that's pretty good," he said. "I think they could use you in the highway department."

The sergeant cackled. "You can say that again."

Hobart looked around at Astrid, mild and pleasant instead of courteously impassive. "Would you mind telling me where your brothers-in-law are working?"

She gave him directions, and he thanked her and got into the car. "Another starting point?" she asked.

"It's like the fingerprints," he said. "We'll try to find out who could, or couldn't, have been around here in that time slot."

"To consider my brothers-in-law at all is so crazy I can't take it seriously."

"This is purely a process of elimination, nothing more." The sergeant started the car. "At present," Hobart added.

When they had driven out, waving back to the boys, she felt as if the house was no longer hers, or had never been hers; the well-mannered strangers going through it, impersonal as robots, turned it into the strange not-always-hostile dwelling found in dreams. She called the boys and went down to work in her garden, finding sanctuary in the feel of warm earth under her knees and in her fingers. The boys looked for worms, tenderly moving them from one spot to another.

"When's Daddy coming home, anyway?" Peter asked suddenly. "I keep wondering."

"Come on over and sit on the front doorstep and talk awhile," Astrid said. "We can smell the narcissus, and look at the water, and maybe a fish hawk will come." She got up off her knees and took a child by each hand and walked to the house. As if her words had conjured them, a pair of ospreys came from the east, calling to each other with short piercing whistles. They wheeled, soared, hovered in space with great beating wings while she held the boys crowded in her lap and told them their father had died in an accident.

It meant little to Chris, though he was as sober and quiet as a small wild animal in its covert. Peter struggled to understand, and, like her, he kept watching the flight and fishing of the ospreys.

"Is he in heaven?" he asked finally. "Can they see him?"

"I think they're too busy catching fish for their babies."

"But he can see *them*, I bet. And *us*. Like Jesus." He twisted around on her knee and looked hard into her face. "Daddy must know Jesus now!"

"I'm sure of it," she said steadily. If Gray was ended for her, who was to prove that the children weren't right? Let them have it their way, to tide them over this moment; she had never been so thankful for their Sunday-school training.

"But I miss him!" Peter cried out suddenly. He pushed his face against her breast and cried. Chris cried in sympathy, and she cried too, into their hair, kissing their hard foreheads, hugging them.

Then it was over. "Let's go in and wash our faces," she said. "We miss him, we always will, but we have to do the best we can."

# Chapter 20

The searchers were in the barn. She hadn't bothered to tell them the gun would never be there, because they would have politely ignored her. But she could remember Gray's coming down the stairs and beginning to tell her where he had put it. Something had interrupted him, Peter, or somebody at the door—anyway, they hadn't got back to it.

In the little space of peace after the weeping on the doorstep, while she washed the children's faces and promised them a row in the dory, she remembered Hobart's original suggestion about the gun. It now seemed entirely possible that Gray had wanted to take the revolver on his long journey, for protection in remote places. He had dug it out of its hiding place, and then it had been used against him and Dorri so they couldn't identify the thieves, who were now murderers.

She wasn't willing to give up the Cades, yet the vivid accounts of their frantic reactions gave her no satisfaction. If I were accused of murder, I'd probably react just the same way, she thought. But it would be so simple if it turned out that they had used Gray's gun against him. At least the legal part would be simple. Then she could be left alone to find her way through her own complexities.

When the men were ready to leave, having found nothing, she told them her idea. They were politely noncommittal. She fixed a lunch and got the fishlines and took the boys out in the dory. The day was blessedly calm and warm, and the dory moved easily over the translucent water. They went outside the cove and around the rocky point where they'd been the other day; this time they could drift among the ledges, watching the eider ducklings. They ate their lunch, and Peter tried to row, but had to give it up. He began talking about the skiff again, and she told him she was going to get a smaller one, just right for him.

Using periwinkles for bait, they fished in the drowsy heat of noon, catching nothing but crabs, which was especially exciting for Chris. One gull paddled patiently around behind the dory, and they named him Sam. It was low tide, so the land loomed over them, and the entrance to the cove was hidden by the chain of high ledges. Even the roof and chimneys of the house had vanished behind a miniature range of hills, which were only mild humps when they were walked upon. It was like being in a different world, alien but safe. The birds, and the ledges themselves, rising like huge bison from larkspur-blue and tourmaline-green shallows, were their friends. She wished she could keep rowing along the shore, always away from the cove, and fetch up in some harbor she had never seen before, like the enchanted scenes she used to discover in jigsaw puzzles.

But nothing remained the same; the tide turned, the wind rose. The southwest breeze begun as a breath was turning fresh. In fifteen minutes it was making ruffles around the ledges and hurrying the dory along. The boys loved it.

"I'll take my new skiff out when it's rough," Peter boasted. They coasted merrily into the cove on a following sea which immediately flattened out into sheltered calm.

"Hi, Kevin!" Chris shouted.

Kevin was standing in an outboard skiff, the engine tilted up on the stern, and he was poling around the wharf, where by now there was very little water under the boat's flat bottom. He poked with the oar at the barnacled pilings, leaned far over to look, poked again.

"He must be looking for crabs," Peter said. He cupped his hands around his mouth and shouted, and this time Kevin heard. He straightened up, waved, and pushed away from the wharf to meet them at the beach. His pleasure at seeing the children again was as obvious as theirs at seeing him. He sat on his heels and listened to them both talking at once.

"I thought you were *sick*," Peter said.

"Not sick," he answered. "I was just getting older." He looked up at Astrid, and she saw in him the man he would become. Then he grinned and said, "I did have some bug, I guess, and everything else did a kung-fu job on me, but . . ." He shrugged. "Here I am."

"Bright-eyed and bushy-tailed!" said Peter, and he and Chris burst into laughter.

"Does your mother know where you are?" Astrid asked. He stood up. "Nope."

"Then you'd better go home, Kevin. I don't want any trouble."

"There won't be any trouble." He sounded like a fully

adult male disposing of a woman's fluttery anxieties. "I know Marm means well, but I was going stir-crazy. She can't see that I'm grown-up now; I know what I know, I saw what I saw, and keeping me shut up in the house and not letting anybody mention anything won't ever wipe it away. I can't keep my mind on this reading I'm supposed to do, and I could kick the TV to pieces. The younger kids look at me as if I've sprouted either wings or horns, I can't tell which."

She had to laugh, to her own surprise. "She's a mother, Kevin. Maybe you're six feet tall with a size-thirteen shoe, but she remembers you the size of Chris. She can't help being protective, it's built in. It goes with the job. Go home, Kevin."

"Not yet," he said stubbornly. He took a pipe out and a package of tobacco from his hip pocket and began to stuff the pipe. The boys shut up and stared. "I started this while I've been in solitary. They didn't say anything. Lesser of two evils, I guess."

"Me being the other one?"

He blushed and immediately lost years. "I didn't mean that!"

"All right, but I want you to go home."

"I have to go, Mama," Chris suddenly announced, jumping up and down.

"Both of you go, over behind the alders. Go on, Peter. You've had your legs crossed for the last five minutes." They went, and Kevin said in a low voice, "Hobart showed up a little while ago. Marm tried to tell him I was too sick to talk, but I strolled in with my pipe and my best sophisticated manner and said, 'How can I help you, Lieutenant?' "

"Well, how could you?"

"He wanted to know more about that night. It looks as if the Cades might be clean, and he kept asking for more details, but I'd already told him everything I could." He took the pipe out of his mouth and frowned at it. "He asked me if I knew anything about a revolver in the house. I asked him if he thought I went through everything while I was taking care of the place. I just got a *look* for that, as if he was thinking about something else."

"He does that awfully well," said Astrid. "Anything more?"

"Nope. Marm went out to the car with him, telling him I was a victim of circumstance, and I went out the back door and down to the shore and took off. None of the other kids were home to give me away."

The boys were coming back, Peter ahead and Chris having trouble with his pants.

"Thank you again for the flowers."

Still scowling at the pipe, he said, "I sent some to Dorri too. It's today. This afternoon. I had to get out of the house, I couldn't sit there imagining it." His voice broke on the end, and he snuffled loudly. She became busy helping Chris with his pants, then straightened Peter out though he indignantly denied the need of it. When she'd finished, Kevin was in control again.

"Tomorrow I'm going back to work."

"Aren't you going away?"

"I can't till this thing's over, and then I won't go. Well, I suppose I'd better head home before Marm starts giving you a hard time. See you later, men," he said to the disappointed boys. He ran down the beach and pushed off the boat.

There were thank-you notes to write for the flowers and to the people who instead sent money, saying, "Get something for the boys," or, candidly, "This should be more useful than flowers right now." *Yes.* The necessity of facing financial details lay ahead like a quicksand; the mere prospect dragged her down. Over coffee that morning Cam had been trying to talk about insurance, Social Security, death benefits, but she'd barely heard him. Sooner or later she'd have to get everything together, when she could bear to. But for now she felt enervated down to her fingertips. It was an effort to move the pen over the notepaper, but she persevered.

On Sunday, they all collected at Fletch's again. His children took the boys on a walk down to Amity Harbor, which gave the adults a chance to talk about the only thing they could talk about these days; weary of it as they were, there was no escape. At least the day was fine and they could be outdoors with a spacious bright blue view of Morgan Bay.

Hobart had been checking the men's alibis; Fletch's, because of his long walks at night, was doubtful. "Seems as if I've got me a reputation as a religious fanatic," he said. "Because I was worried about my brother's soul. I don't know if I can convince 'em that I'm concerned about my own soul too and that I don't spill blood, innocent or otherwise." He spoke as slowly as he ever did. How could he keep himself on a leash like that, Astrid wondered. "Sure I've been upset, as much by myself as by anyone else. I felt so savage that I had to get off by myself and wrestle with my own devils. I admit to murder in my heart—"

"Don't let Hobart hear you say that!" Cam exploded.

Fletch half smiled. "But not in deed," he went on. "And if you don't think that murder in your heart is hell enough, I hope you never have to find out."

"It's all foolishness!" Nora's ebullience had taken a beating, and she was looking dark around the eyes. "They don't *know* that it was that night."

"What difference does it make?" asked Fletch. "I've been out walking almost every night."

"Well, the Gardeners came to our place that night to watch a special on Australia with us, because we have color," Harriet said. "So that clears Cam."

"Only till midnight," said Cam. "But nobody knows what time it might have happened. I don't know whether it'll be a help or a hindrance to have that gun show up. Dollars to doughnuts it won't have a print on it. So Hobart can line us up and go eeny-meeny-miney-mo—"

"Cam, stop that!" Harriet cried out suddenly. She was ready to cry, and he went to her quickly and put his arms around her. Astrid's nose prickled. She could embrace and comfort the boys, but who would embrace and comfort *her?* Who would belong to *her?*

"Well, I think this talk has gone on long enough," said Nora. "We're all honest decent people, and the truth will prevail."

"I've got a new subject," Astrid began brightly. Then she remembered that it was connected with the old one, but she had to go on with it. "I'd like to get a small skiff for Peter, and soon. Does anybody know where I can buy one?"

Cam and Fletch both answered eagerly on that; they had

ideas, they would start looking at once. Cam even went inside to call up one man, but he was gone for the day. "Never mind," he told Astrid. "He'll be in tonight."

"That boy'll have his skiff in a week," said Fletch solemnly, "if I have to build it myself."

On Monday morning she recognized Hobart's car coming in, and she sent the boys up to tidy their room before they could see the car and go out to meet it. She met the officer on the back porch. He was alone this time. "You have no right to accuse my brothers-in-law of anything!" She was poised and exhilarated with indignation.

He didn't seem surprised by the attack. "Weren't they outraged at the way your husband treated you and disgraced the family's good name? Isn't Fletcher Price in particular very strong against sin, and so forth?"

"So am I! So are you, or you *should* be! And do you think that if Fletch ever did anything like that, if he went out of his head and a gun was handy, and he never owned a gun, whether you believe it or not..." She lost track, which was frightening, and put her hands to her head. "Oh," she said softly.

"Do you have anything to take?" he asked.

"Not for that," she said.

He sat on the railing. "Then go on about your brother-in-law."

"He would never do what those killers did. Leave them there like that for me to find, or even the children. He'd have given himself up at once."

"You people are very loyal to each other."

It made her wonder what he had been asking about her.

She said, "Cam curses and blows off steam, but that's all it is. He's no more a killer than Fletch is."

The boys pushed open the screen door and came out. "Hello!" Peter exclaimed happily. He was carrying his frog.

"Hello," said Hobart. "What's the frog's name?"

"Jolly Frog, like in the song." He sang the first line, ready to do the whole production, but Astrid stopped him. Peter said hurriedly, "He swims across the river where all the sweet music is, and he's going to be a dancer in yellow."

"Someday," Hobart said, "you can sing it all for me. It sounds like a good one. What have *you* got?" he asked Chris.

"A owl. His name's Mr. Rollins." This was new to Astrid, who thought, I must tell George.

"Look out he doesn't catch the frog."

Chris's eyes widened with delighted speculation, but Peter said patronizingly, "He's too small."

"I'd like to talk to you," Hobart said to Astrid. "Can they play on their sand pile there? We could sit here on the steps so you can keep an eye on them, if you want."

"All right," she answered. The boys didn't need to be watched that closely, but she couldn't stand another discussion inside the kitchen; the very thought gave her claustrophobia. Lately she had been remembering the days when Gray was remodeling the kitchen, so that he almost seemed to be still working there while they talked about his dead body.

"Let's get back to this note," he began. It was like a punch in the ribs.

"What about it?" Don't sound hostile, she warned herself.

"You're positive they never got here."

"Yes!" Too sharp. She was suddenly frightened.

"You're very strong, aren't you, Mrs. Price? You row a lot, you probably swim, you chop wood—"

"What are you getting at?" she demanded.

"We're just going about the process of elimination, Mrs. Price." He didn't look up. "Would you feel better if you had your lawyer here?"

"Why should I need him? Are you about to read me my rights?" She tried to sound amused, but it was a failure.

He said with annoying impassivity, "Not at all. I'd like to check a few facts with you. You are strong, aren't you?"

"No more than most of the women around here. We're all pretty competent."

"You could take a healthy young girl by the throat and pin her against a car."

She groaned. "Oh, Lord. *That!* I found her at my car showing the boys her diamond ring and telling them their daddy was going to marry her. The obscene phone calls had been directed at *me*, but when my children were touched, it was the last straw. I'd had it."

"Obscene phone calls?" he asked softly.

"Yes. I was able to stop those when I went to Gray— my husband about them. Then she began tearing down the hill into the yard here in this sports car he bought, racing around, blowing the horn, ripping out again. I could stop that too."

"We know about it."

"I'm sure you do."

"And then on Main Street in Williston you reached the last straw. There was a confrontation, she shouted an obscenity at you and made the finger sign, and you took her by the throat and slapped her face."

"Yes, afterwards I was upset because I'd forgotten myself that far, and I decided it was time I got away for a while. I was able to rent this cottage in Parmenter for two weeks."

"She'd already told her mother and other people that she was afraid of you, and after the incident on Main Street she said you'd threatened to kill her."

"I know we're not supposed to speak ill of the dead," said Astrid, "but Dorri was a liar."

"She'd been harassing you, humiliating you, and you'd been under weeks of strain, and when she finally got to your children you blew up. Is that right? In your own words, you'd had it."

"I grabbed her and slapped her. She had it coming to her. But that's as far as I went, Lieutenant." She said it quietly, not really believing that he could suspect her. When he talked to the children about the frog and the owl, there'd been a glimpse of the unofficial man, a man who wouldn't ever believe that she, or Cam, or Fletch would hurt Gray.

"Let's get back to the note. You wanted to talk with your husband. You'd been saying right along that you wouldn't divorce him. You told her mother that; you told your husband's family—"

She sat stiffly forward and he said, "They're as loyal to you as you are to them. They've only been trying to help, Mrs. Price. . . . Would you mind telling me what you wanted to talk to him about?"

She felt like a lost hunter going in circles with a snowy night coming on, thinking, This can't be happening to *me*. "There are a lot of things to talk about when you have a home together and children."

"Like asking him to come back? But instead of coming alone to see you, he brought the girl. . . . You're sure you don't have any idea where that revolver is, Mrs. Price?"

"No," she said, getting up. "Will you leave?" She was trembling on the edge of flying apart. He stood up too, looking gravely down at her. "We'll be in touch," he said and walked to the car.

"Goodbye, goodbye!" the children called. "Come again!"

Terror chased incredulity round and round. She saw herself railroaded, accused, unable to prove she didn't shoot them and drag their bodies up into the fishhouse loft. . . . *You're very strong, aren't you?* Not able to dispose of them any other way, she hoped to "discover" them as mysterious homicides.

She could see the whole mind-blowing, bowel-churning process. Booking. Court. She would be separated from the boys. Any jury would say she had plenty of motive and opportunity. They could not look into her face and see the truth, any more than Hobart could at four feet away. His blue eyes were blind, *blind*.

It was always said that the state bore the burden of proof. The state had to prove you were guilty; you didn't have to prove your innocence. But you did, you *did!* And what it all came down to was that she was completely alone.

The telephone rang, and she raced for it. "Are you all right?" asked Dinah. "You sound funny."

"I'm just tired, Dine."

"We wanted you and the boys over for a cook-out to-night."

"They'd love it. I'll see how I feel later."

"I wish there was somebody staying with you," Dinah fretted.

"I'd have to talk when I didn't feel like it. . . . I'll call you later, after I've had a nap this afternoon."

She was tempted to call Nora, or to drive to where the men were working, just to say the words *They think I did it*. But that would make them indelible. How could she go to the cook-out and act as if this hadn't happened to her? She was going to suffocate from pure fear. She took one of the relaxers, but it did nothing and she was afraid to take another one. She thought wildly of taking the boys and running away, but she'd get nowhere.

And why, *why?* Her mind raged over it while the boys took their naps. Why me? What have *I* done? I've lost my Gray; is that my sin, my crime?

After the boys' naps she took them out in the dory and rowed them around for over an hour. Her frightened heart and aroused system pumped frantic energy through her body. What will I do, what will I do? she kept thinking.

She had to go home finally. Chris's eyes were glazing, his thumb in his mouth. Peter kept rubbing his hands through his hair.

*Would you feel better if you had your lawyer here?* Oh, he'd known very well what he was about. Worn out now, she surrendered to the idea.

# Chapter
# 21

**K**evin was coming down through the field as she beached the dory, and he ran the rest of the way and swung the boys out over the bow. "Hi, men! You been on a sea voyage?" Revived, they began telling him what they'd seen. Astrid kept busy fastening the painter into the loop of the haul-off line until he took the line away from her and pulled the dory out to the crosspiece.

As usual the boys had to run around behind the alders. "I hope Chris makes it," she said, trying to sound amused.

"Are you all right, Astrid?" Kevin asked. "It's none of my business, but you kind of worry me."

"I kind of worry me too. Lieutenant Hobart kind of worries me most of all."

"*Why?*" He reddened. "What's he bugging you for?"

"Because I had motive and opportunity."

"Well, Geezuss!" He stopped himself, looking toward the alders, and spoke more softly. "So have I! So have plenty of other people! Hey, what about deer-jackers? Supposing Gray caught 'em at it, and they had it in for him, anyway?"

"They can't go out and just haul people in. So all I have to do is try to keep from jumping out of my skin with nerves while the law makes up its mind." Talking about it now let off a little of the pressure.

The boys returned, and she had to adjust Chris's minute shorts. "I'm going to fix supper for the boys," she said. "Want a sandwich?" His mother's disapproval was insignificant right now.

"I'm not hungry, but I'll keep you company. You look like you could use some. I'm better than nothing."

"You're a lot better than nothing, believe me."

When they got to the house Dinah was calling. "I forgot," Astrid apologized. "I think I'm going to bed when the boys do, I'm that tired. Thanks just the same. I appreciate the thought."

"We're thinking about you all the time. I just wish there was something real and positive we could do."

Like finding a murderer, Astrid thought. "Just helping out with the children now and then counts," she said. "And being a friend."

Conversation at the table had to be safe for the boys. In one day back at work Kevin had gathered up a great deal of local gossip which wasn't about her; it was strange to realize that other existences went on.

When Kevin got up to go, he said blithely, "Well, now I'm off to ask some questions about jackers."

"Now look, Kevin," she told him. "I'm going to call my lawyer in the morning, and let him worry for me. You won't do me any favor by getting involved."

"I'm already involved. Don't worry, I'm not going charging into the barracks, telling them what they ought to do. I can do it myself." The telephone rang. "That may be my mother," he said grimly. "I'm not here, so you won't have to lie for me."

He went off the porch in a long, sailing leap, much admired by the boys, and into his car. Astrid answered the telephone. It was Celia Whitehouse, both harassed and imperious. "Is my son there?"

"No, he is not, Celia," Astrid said coldly and hung up. The rudeness went against her grain; she felt uneasy, even guilty, and then saw the irony of that in her present situation.

Still, she felt slightly better than before Kevin's arrival, like someone adrift in a life raft seeing the lights of a distant ship; there was a faint hope of being seen. You couldn't tell what Kevin might turn up or start in motion.

She hadn't thought of night hunters before, and apparently the police hadn't, either. But it could be. Gray, who didn't even hunt legally, especially hated jackers. It didn't have to be the ones he'd caught so long ago. There was a new dimension of violence to rural crime now. Last year a poacher had pulled a gun on a warden and might have shot him if his more sensible friend hadn't disarmed him from behind.

When the boys were asleep she cried hard into her pillow for a long time, as if her Gray had been returned to her and then destroyed before they could even embrace.

She woke up at her usual time with the dawn chorus, rested enough to wonder quite dispassionately if Lieutenant Hobart would be around bright and early this morning to read her her rights. *You have the right to remain silent.* Could any Old Testament pronouncement be more blood-chilling? It gave you permission not to scream on the rack.

She felt as if half her life had been spent drinking strong coffee before dawn. It would be hours before she could call her lawyer. She could imagine his nice friendly face turning dismayed. *I don't handle criminal cases, Mrs. Price.*

*But I'm not a criminal!*

*Nevertheless, you'll need a different lawyer.*

Then, hopelessly, *Can you recommend one?* Her objectivity plunged to earth like a murdered bird. I can call Fletch and Cam; they'll come running. They'll know what to do. . . . I ought to, anyway. Prepare them for the shock. . . . She began to feel wild again and fought against it, trying to make plans for the boys. Maybe there'd be bail—there *ought* to be bail where it was all circumstantial. She didn't know how it worked, but she could put the place up as her security, maybe. . . .

"Oh God," she whispered. How many people had begun, *Oh God, if there is a God. . . .* A fine time to go crawling and sniveling to Him now.

A little after seven, while the children were still sleeping heavily, Hobart's car drove into the yard. Again he was alone. She met him outside, coldly braced. He wore the blue tie, and she was glad that she was neatly dressed and brushed to meet the end of the world.

"Whatever you've come to say, please don't say it until after I've called my lawyer."

"You won't need your lawyer," he said gravely. "We have a witness to the fact that your husband and Dorri Sears were alive long after you were back at the farm in Parmenter."

She began to tremble, her face felt cold, her head was swimming. He took her by the elbow. "You'd better sit down. Do you want to go inside?"

"Yes—the boys might wake up." She didn't know if she'd make it into the kitchen, but she did with his hand firmly holding her elbow.

"I wanted to let you know as soon as possible," he said, "without waking you with a telephone call in the middle of the night."

"I wouldn't have minded," she said. "Is this a real witness? I mean there's no chance of a mistake?"

"No, she's sure of her facts. It's a girl named Mavis Carter, one of Dorri's chums. Dorri called her up that night sometime between eleven and twelve and said she was here." He added dryly, "She'd bragged that she'd make it, so she called her friend to prove it. She was giggling, and he must have taken the phone away and hung up."

"Did Mavis come forward with this? I'm trying to get it straight."

"Not on her own. She didn't know it was important till the Whitehouse boy got to her. He brought her over to the barracks last night. I was back in Orono, but Sergeant Whittaker questioned her pretty thoroughly. She even named a couple of girls she'd called immediately after the Sears girl called *her*."

"Will you have a cup of coffee?" she said. "Or is that drinking on duty?" She was beginning to feel a little drunk. "It wouldn't be bribery, anyway. Not now."

"Hardly. Thanks, I'd like one."

"Toast?"

"Just the coffee, thanks."

"How did Kevin ever catch on? He tore out of here talking about jackers."

"I guess he had a brainstorm. He said the girl was a telephone addict, and he wondered if they'd had time to get into the house and if she'd called anyone. Seems that he heard of her brags too, and he knew the Carter girl was a special friend. So he followed his hunch."

"He was too decent to tell me about it, but he didn't forget it," she said softly.

"When I talked to him at his home the other day, he said he was your friend. I guess he is."

The boys were stirring, and he got up to leave. "Thank you for the cup of coffee. It's the best one I've had for a long time."

"Mine tasted awfully good too." She remembered something which tried to suffocate her relief. "What about Fletch and Cam?"

"Well, they're safe until midnight, and after that it's their wives' word that'll count. There's nothing we can do about that, even if we wanted to."

"Then thank you for all the good news. When Gr—my husband died like that, I thought it was the end of the world, but when I thought I might lose the boys . . ." Her throat clamped shut.

"They're great youngsters," he said quickly. "Yesterday wasn't personal, I hope you understand that."

"Yes, I do." Today she understood everything. They smiled faintly at each other, then he became official again.

"We'll keep on looking. Kevin may be right about poachers. We've had to let the Cades go on the homicide charge, for lack of evidence, though we've gathered quite a bit of useful material on other charges."

"That's some gain then, I suppose." She walked out on the porch with him and watched him go. He put his arm out and waved when he made the turn up into the lane. Then she went in to attend to the boys. Her long weeping the night before and the news this morning had combined to give her a sensation of both looseness and freedom, not quite euphoria, but something better than what she'd experienced for a long time. It was a glimpse, narrow, niggardly, but valid, of a possible life ahead in which she would not forever be hurt, depressed, degraded, and frightened by what had happened to her and Gray. Nothing could ever make up to her and the boys for the loss of him, but they would survive and find something good, somehow.

In a little while she'd call Nora and say, "I hear we're all in the clear." For now she wanted to make use of this new wellspring of energy. She'd been merely keeping the dishes washed and the floor swept, now she'd really clean up. When the boys had gone out to their sand pile, she went upstairs and stripped their beds and vacuumed the room. From there she went into hers and Gray's and stood looking around. She could change the colors and rearrange the furniture, put that bed into the spare room and bring in the narrower one, set her mother's small desk by the window with a good lamp . . . She would have to write her mother now; she would call it an accident, trusting that scandal and murder in a tiny coastal village in Maine would never make the papers outside the state. If her mother swooped down on them for Christmas—she was capable of sudden attacks of devotion—Astrid would be prepared to give her a good story, and the family would back her up, she was sure. They wouldn't have to lie, just say it was too painful to discuss, and her mother had never had friends in the village who would sympathetically mention the tragedy as if she knew all about it.

The boys' engine noises rose to her like the spring calls of some exotic creatures. Then she began to strip the double bed in preparation for taking it apart and moving it.

A car came down the lane, and this time her ribs didn't seem to clamp like a torture instrument around her lungs and squeeze her heart. It wouldn't be Lieutenant Hobart; he had no more business with her. She went to look out, folding the prismatic quilt as she went. It was Kevin's car, and the boys were shrieking, "Hi, Kevin!"

"Hello, men. What's new?"

"Good morning, Kevin!" she called down to him. "Why aren't you at work?"

"I'm on my way. Just stopped by to see if the Loot's been here yet." He looked up at her, shading his eyes against the sun.

"He sure has, and I don't know how I can thank you. Come on in. I'll be right down as soon as I finish here." She left the window and tossed the pillows into a chair, and took off blankets and sheets in one mighty heave. Instead of the mattress pad she expected, there was an old quilt which she had last seen folded away in the blanket chest; she used it under the sheets in winter to make the bed warmer. She stared at it, thinking in consternation, If I put that on without knowing it, I *have* been way out. But I never use it in summer! ... And she remembered suddenly how the bed had felt too hot on her first night home from Parmenter, but she'd thought the heat was in herself.

Kevin called from the foot of the stairs. "I've only

got a minute—I just wanted to be sure you had the scoop."

She didn't answer. Cold-handed, slow, but in a process as irrevocable as a walk to the scaffold, she turned back the quilt. There was nothing on the mattress, but she could tell that it had been turned.

"Astrid?" Kevin questioned from the stairs. There was a light, high quality in his voice, as if he had scarcely any breath.

She seized the grips on the side of the heavy innerspring mattress and gave it a mighty heave half off the box spring; then she stood it up on its side and looked at what had been hidden. The brownish stains were not plentiful, but they were there, where the blood must have seeped through the mattress pad.

There was a dreadful clamor in her head, in spite of the silence in the house, so that she didn't hear Kevin on the stairs. But there he was, his head almost touching the top of the frame. He was gazing desolately at the mattress, and then he turned those sad eyes on her.

"*Were* they making love in this bed, Kevin?" she asked very softly. The clamor had died away. The engine noises from the sand pile went on in the warm stillness.

Kevin shook his head. "No. She'd turned back the bed-clothes and she was sitting on the edge, and he went in and told her to get out of there and come on." It was as mechanical as a computer voice. "And she said, Oh please, Gray, just once, and he said *No*, you wanted to go, by God you're going right now, and she saw me in the door-way and she laughed and I shot her. And when he saw her fall back he started to turn and I shot him, and he fell over on her. And I left them a while. I was trying to think what to do, so that's how come the blood. She didn't bleed much, but he did, a lot. Later I took the sheets and the mattress pad away and buried them in the swamp down behind my house."

She knew her lips were moving but she couldn't say anything. She tried painfully to think of something. Finally, with relief, she remembered. "It wasn't just a hunch about her calling Mavis."

"No, I heard her."

"Why don't you tell me from the beginning, Kevin?" she suggested. He seemed earnestly willing to cooperate; he frowned as if he were trying to get everything exactly right. He put his hands over his head and held onto the door casing, lanky and young and not at all terrible.

"I was driving back that night and when I was coming around the curve past the end of Lowell's pasture I saw a car turn into this road. I thought it was the Cades, or some other bums. I parked up on the road and walked down. I had the gun, and I was going to hold them and call the police."

"What gun was that, Kevin?" she asked gently.

"Yours," he answered as if she should have known. "I found it all wrapped up in an old wooden cigar box on top of that wardrobe in the attic. There were shells with it, too. I kept it with me in case I met up with the Cades sometime."

Kevin, of all people, hunting through the secret places of her house! As if that mattered now when Kevin, of all people, had killed Gray. It was too enormous a truth for ordinary emotions.

"Wow, was I excited!" he said in a weird parody of himself. "I thought, Here's my chance! But then I saw the Audi instead and the house all lighted up. I went up on the porch. Dorri was going through all the kitchen cupboards and drawers, and she read the notes on the telephone pad, and she had this little smirk all the time, and she was singing to herself. Then she went into the hall and yelled upstairs, What are you doing up there? Are you still packing?"

It was becoming most horribly real. Astrid moved to take hold of one of the bedposts to help brace her, while she watched Gray up here and Dorri down there.

"He said, Yes, and she said, You're taking too long. I'm coming up, and he said, real sharp, No! Don't come up! And she laughed and said, Can't I look in her closet? And he said, No, you can't. I'll be right down." The desolation came over him again. He dropped his hands and slumped against the side of the doorframe. "If she'd only obeyed him. But you can't—couldn't ever tell her *don't*. She went up anyway. She shouldn't have. You know what I mean, don't you, Astrid?"

"I think so. What did you do then?"

"I went into the kitchen and across the hall into the living room. Gray came down with his case and told her to come too, and she said, In a minute. He went out and put his bag in the Audi. I watched him from the window. He was real tense and nervous. Then I heard her dialing and talking to Mavis and laughing up a storm. I went up the stairs and into the spare room and listened to her. She was making her brags come true, she said. She was turning back the covers while she was talking. She said Gray didn't want to, but she knew how to make him."

He was ashamed, turning his head away, then giving her a sidewise look while the color ran darkly into his cheek. "He came running up the stairs and took her by surprise,

I could tell he grabbed the telephone and slammed it down, and then she began coaxing him, and I was afraid it was going to happen—I knew I couldn't stand it if it did," he said pleadingly. "So I went to let them know I was there."

"And you still had the gun."

"Yes, but I was only going to scare them. I thought maybe I could even break them up for good if I threatened them. And then she saw me and she laughed and said, Well, look who's here! Cute Kevin the—I shot her before she could say whatever she was going to say, and then him."

Her legs were trembling and she lowered herself cautiously to sit on the edge of the box spring; she had a good view of the bloodstains, so she turned away and stared at the sun-filled windows. Gray's blood.

"I went downstairs and tried to think what to do," he said. "I didn't know what to do with them. I had to get them out of sight, so I lugged them down and put them in the skiff, and I kept thinking I'd get rid of them later. I threw the gun off the wharf. I put the sheets and the mattress pad in a plastic trash bag. I drove the Audi over to North Applecross and parked it in the woods, then I walked back, just inside the trees most of the way, and where there weren't trees I dived for the bushes whenever I heard a car. There were only a few, that time of night. I had that plastic bag, you see. It was kind of nutty to take it with me, but I wasn't thinking too straight."

"I can see that," said Astrid. The bright light shimmered in her eyes. The engine noises still went reassuringly on, relentless as cicadas in August.

"When I came by my house I took a short cut we kids have down into the swamp and buried the bag in a deep place I know about, with rocks on it. Then I came back here and drove my car in. I was some tired and dry and hungry. I couldn't get over being *hungry* after what I'd done, but I was." He sounded as if he expected her to marvel at it too. "And those damn Cades had been here! They must have beat it when they heard me coming. But they never got into the fishhouse, because I'd locked that and I had the key."

"You were looking for the gun the other day when we came in," Astrid said.

"Yep, but I guess it's really sunk down in the mud now." He came around to stand between her and the window. "Astrid, you'll have to believe me, I never meant to—" To kill them, she expected him to say. But he went on. "To leave them there. I kept trying to think how to get rid of them. But it was like I was paralyzed every time I faced it. Trying to block it out. Then you came back, and you kept talking about getting that skiff down, and I got sick. *Really* sick."

"But you came back to do it."

"Well, I figured they had to be found, and I might's well be the one. Astrid, they deserved it for doing what they did to you and to me. Can't you see it? But I never planned it. It was like an explosion in my head."

"I can believe that, Kevin. I've felt the same way."

"So you won't tell!"

"I'm hoping you will, Kevin."

"No!" he shouted. "I can breathe now! I still love her, but she can't laugh at me any more, or at you either." He plunged out of the room and down the stairs.

# Chapter
# 22

She ran down the stairs behind him, hardly touching the treads, buoyant as a lifting balloon. The screen door slammed, the children hailed him.

"Kevin, wait!" she shouted, bursting out onto the porch. But he was past the sand pile and running by the far corner of the barn, toward the woods. The trucks were toppled in the sand pile and he had a child under each arm, and he looked as if he could run forever. She jumped from the top step and went sprinting after them. She'd always been a good runner in school, but that was a long time ago, and Kevin ran every day of his life. She couldn't remember to breathe properly; a stitch went into her side like a dagger and she couldn't suck air down her aching throat. The boys' laughter came back to her as they were carried off into the woods and then the sound was suddenly cut off.

Sobbing painfully, she toiled toward the wall of spruces. Her eyes felt afire; sweat ran down her back. She heard herself crying, "Gray, Gray, the children!"

"*Stop that*," she said wheezily but audibly. It gave her a second wind to get into the damp, resinous shade of the woods. A squirrel broke into explosive sputterings overhead. She didn't know which way to move; she could hear nothing but the squirrel, which came down a trunk to curse her at close range.

"He would never hurt the children," she said, and the squirrel quieted for a moment to listen, then began again. She left the woods and ran back to the house. With her hand on the telephone she stopped to think. Police cruisers gathering, volunteers who'd heard the alert on their scanners showing up to help hunt—it could pitch him over the brink if he weren't dangling there already. And he had her children.

"He would never hurt them," she repeated to herself, like an oath. She called George Rollins's home, and his wife said he'd gone to haul but she could reach him by CB radio if it was an emergency. "It is," Astrid told her, keeping from a shout. Then she called Dinah.

"Could you come over without your children? But bring Poochie? My kids have wandered off, and he might be able to help."

"I'll be right there, but let me get the word around! There's plenty of people available to help!"

"No, Dine. You'll know why when you get here."

She went out past the barn again and stood staring at the woods and listening. The summer silence, spangled with birdsong as the sun spangled the shade in the woods, had an evil quality, like a diabolical consciousness. Its spell was broken by the sound of an engine in the cove, and she ran around the house and saw George Rollins's boat coming. She raced down to meet him, and when she tried to tell him she couldn't.

"Take a breath," he counseled her. "Now just nod. Is it the children?"

She nodded, her eyes on his.

"*Drowned?*"

She shook her head wildly, found her voice.

"Taken! He ran into the woods!"

George started for the house. "I'll have to call the police." She dragged at his arm.

"If we could find him, quietly—George, he won't hurt the children *now*, but if he's cornered and scared to death, he could."

George stopped in his stride and glared down at her. "Who, for God's sake?"

"Kevin."

His head jolted back as if he'd been struck. "Oh, my Jesus," he said softly. Then he walked faster, taking her along with him. "Listen, I have to call Hobart, but he'll manage it the right way. I'll be talking on your phone, so the scanners won't pick me up. Astrid, I *have* to. It's my duty!"

She let him go into the house and she went out and stood by the barn again. Dinah's station wagon came down the lane in a noisy rush, scattering gravel. She leaped out, and Poochie behind her, cavorting with pleasure, ran at once to the sand pile where he smelled all the trucks, the frog and the owl, and Peter's sweater. "Find Peter," Dinah said to him. "Find Peter." Poochie leaped to kiss her face, then smelled the sweater she thrust at him. He sniffed all around the sand pile and the barn doors, arriving finally at the kitchen door, wagging his tail at the sound of George's voice inside.

"Oh, Poochie, you're no bloodhound," Dinah sighed. "Listen, Astrid, where have you looked? Be calm now. They're just out of sight somewhere, that's all."

"They're in the woods." She pointed. "And I forgot, he was carrying them. The dog couldn't pick up a trail anyway." She felt about to cry.

"*Who* was carrying them?"

"Kevin. He did it, Dinah. He just told me the whole story, and then he grabbed the boys and ran."

Dinah's freckles stood out dark, and she was stumbling all over her words. "Now listen, dear, he'd never hurt them. They may be just inside the woods someplace. We'll take my dumb dog up there, and—"

George came out. "They're locating Hobart, and I made it clear we can't take chances on panicking this kid. They can quietly surround the area, believe me, Astrid. They're going ahead with it now."

"Thanks, George. Now Dine and I are taking Poochie up to the woods, and Peter's sweater, to see what we can do." She knew he and Dinah were exchanging signals, but this was no time to be furious or humiliated or insist she wasn't a nut case.

"Don't you want Nora to come over?" he asked her. "She could get hold of Fletch and Cam too."

"I'll get them if I need them. Come on, Dine. Here, Poochie." Poochie pranced around her and made a foolish leap after a butterfly. "Good boy, Poochie!" she applauded him. "We'll show 'em, won't we?"

Dinah caught up with her; George sat down on the steps and lit a cigarette.

Poochie had a splendid time in the woods. Finally, when offered another sniff at the sweater, he grabbed it and ran, shook it violently, growling the whole time, and then attempted to put it to death. Dinah wrestled it away from him. "He's no good," she said in despair, "and we're just messing it up for dogs that are really trained to search."

"He couldn't carry them indefinitely," Astrid argued. "They're good healthy chunks of boy. He's had to put them down somewhere. I keep feeling I'll go around some big boulder and find them."

"Well, it won't be through Poochie. He'll only find them if you point them out to him."

Astrid sensed rather than heard a stirring in one of the growths of bracken, shadbush, moosewood, and wild cherry that filled old cuttings in the spruce forest. She took Poochie by the collar and gestured Dinah to be silent. They both stared at the sunstruck hollow of pastel greens; someone was moving cautiously around in there, and in another instant they would see. But Poochie saw too and let out one suspicious woof.

"Stay where you are," a masculine voice ordered. A sheriff's deputy broke out through the tall bracken and looked at them with quizzical exasperation.

"I don't know if you two ladies are aware that we're searching these woods for three persons. It would be better if you left. And the dog," he added. Poochie looked pleased by the special mention.

"This woman is the mother of the missing children," Dinah said coldly. The deputy said to Astrid, "I'm sorry, ma'am, but I still think it would be better if you left the area, just in case."

"In case of what?" Astrid asked. "If I can find the children first, *that's* what would be better."

"There'll be no shooting," said the deputy. "We have instructions not to harm him in any way." He stood there like a tree and was just as impervious.

"Come on, Astrid," Dinah said, taking her by the arm. "How many men are out?" she asked the deputy.

"At least a dozen, and we've got watchers at strategic points. He's on foot, he can't go far." He allowed himself an encouraging nod at Astrid. "It'll work out all right, ma'am."

She let Dinah start her back the way they'd come. Poochie was fully capable of following this fresh trail and went along nose to the ground, tail telegraphing his enthusiasm. "We'll get something to eat," Dinah was saying, the way Astrid talked to the children. "And who knows, maybe they're back already! What d'you bet?"

Astrid didn't bother to answer. They'd taken a long circuitous way over mossy slopes and down steps of ledge into hollows, they'd peered behind every glacial boulder, and on the way back Poochie repeated all the motions. Dinah would have hurried him on, but Astrid said, "Let him. The longer we take, the more chance of their being home when we get there."

She spoke without conviction. She was very tired. It wasn't quite noon, but the search seemed to have been going on for a week. They came out on a flat shelf of ledge thrust out like a rustic stage or the broad forward deck of a ship, and through a break in the trees they could look down on the distant green-yellow sea of the meadow, the barn weathervane and house chimneys, the blue shimmer of the cove at midday.

With a sigh Astrid said, "Well, let's go on." Suddenly Poochie shot off to the left and down over tumbled, lichened blocks, dashed up a mossy slope, and disappeared under low-hanging spruce boughs.

"Squirrel, fox, rabbit," said Dinah in resignation. "Let's hope it's not a porcupine." She whistled and then said, "Oh come on, he'll show up."

"No," said Astrid. "Let's follow." She was off, jumping down the way the dog had gone, skidding on the damp moss, crawling under the branches.

She heard the boys before she saw them, they were laughing so hard while Poochie washed faces and ears. They were in a little natural shelter formed by slabs of rock heaved up by tree roots.

And they were alone except for Poochie. He was holding Chris down now and giving his ears a going-over. "Hi, Mama, hi, Aunt Dine!" Peter was positively debonair about it. "You found Kevin yet?"

"No, not yet." Astrid restrained herself from seizing them both at once. Besides, Dinah had to get Poochie away from Chris first.

"Oh boy, he's hiding good," Peter said proudly. "We hid good too."

"You sure did," said Dinah. "Chris, your hair's full of spruce spills."

Astrid sat on the ground and pulled Chris into her lap and brushed spills away with one hand, unnecessarily dusted off Peter's seat with the other, just to touch him.

"So that's what the game is," she said, smiling. "Hide-and-go-seek."

"Yup. Kevin told us not to move or we'd get lost. And he said not to holler. He said if it took a long time to find us, we'd get a prize. Do we get one, Mama?" he asked greedily.

"You do."

"Oh, boy! Hi, Poochie!" He hugged the dog.

"Poochie should get a prize," said Astrid, "because he found you."

"I'll bet even Poochie can't find Kevin because he knows lots of good places."

"Let's go back home and find out."

Lieutenant Hobart met them halfway across the field. "Anybody tired?" he asked casually and hoisted Chris up to his shoulder. Chris looked dazzled. Peter ran to take hold of his other hand, talking excitedly about the game.

Astrid began, "Have you found—?"

He shook his head. "And the Whitehouses are here."

"Oh Lord," groaned Dinah.

Astrid said, "If they're as worried about their boy as I was about mine, I don't care what she says to me, Dine."

But Kevin's mother was sitting in her car, up on the lane. Astrid and Dinah took the children and dog into the house. Nora and Harriet were in the kitchen, making tea and coffee and sandwiches. The greetings were quiet, almost reverent, and nobody let the boys think it had been anything else but some marvelous game. Chris was sleepy, but Peter was radiantly wide awake, waiting for the moment when Kevin would be found.

Cam, Fletch, Kevin's father, and George Rollins were all out in the search party. Dinah took the boys into the bathroom to wash up, Nora carried a cup of tea out to Celia Whitehouse, and Harriet put food in front of Astrid, who could only drink.

Sipping coffee, she told Hobart about the scene with Kevin. "He can deny it completely, you know," he said.

She shrugged. "Everything has been so awful that now

I don't really care. I just want to run away and stop thinking. He said that Kevin would get over it. But he didn't."

Hobart didn't ask her who *he* was. He went outside, and she went to lie down on the living-room sofa and tried to relax, wondering just how many yards of muscle made up the human body and knowing that every inch of hers was twitching and quivering. Poochie came in and lay on the rug beside her. She rested her hand on his frowsty head, and he sighed deeply and fell asleep. From afar she heard Dinah talking over lunch with the boys, telling them the prizes would be awarded later, after their naps. People came and went in the dooryard; voices were muted, and no one came near her.

Suddenly she knew she was waking up, and she didn't know how long she had slept or what had happened in that time. But it had been only about a half hour. Poochie had left her and was in the kitchen with Dinah, who sat in the rocker reading the *Patriot*, her feet on the cold stove hearth.

"The boys are asleep, and I'm trying to tranquilize myself." She made a face. "Nothing's happened. I really think he may have done away with himself, Astrid. It would solve a lot of problems, wouldn't it?"

"Not for his father and mother." She went to the door and saw Celia's car still part way up the lane. She felt as if she'd had a much longer sleep, at least she was stronger in the body and clearer in the head. "Wherever he is, he'll never come out with everybody waiting to pounce."

Lieutenant Hobart came in. "I've had some men searching the Whitehouses' alder swamp for the plastic bag, and it's been found. He hadn't hidden it very well."

"If everyone would go away," she said, "Kevin might come back here."

It startled even him. His black eyebrows went up. "You mean you want to risk a repetition?"

"I'm not *that* crazy. No, if somebody like George Rollins stayed here, out of sight in the house, but everybody else was gone, including his mother, he might come back. You see, he thinks we're both victims."

"I'm staying too," Dinah said. "I'll hide in the cellar if you want me to, but I'm staying."

"Well, I think we should move the search anyway," Hobart said, sounding almost indulgent. "He's probably miles away by now. Leaving the children like that was a delaying action; he hoped everybody'd be looking for them first."

He went out to talk with Mrs. Whitehouse. Some of the searchers were using walkie-talkies, and after the next check, the center of the search was moved to the Whitehouse property. Kevin could have gone miles through fairly dense woods without being spotted and might now be feeling safe in the family woodlot, or on his way to the alder swamp to retrieve the plastic bag and hide it somewhere else.

Sometime during the morning George had taken his lobster boat home and returned in his radio-equipped car. Now this was driven out by one of the deputies. Cam and Fletch and their wives left, though they would go only as far as the harbor and wait at Dinah's house for news. Hobart left finally, making it clear this was against his better judgment.

"Why, if you're so sure he's on his home ground by now?" Astrid asked.

"Because I could be wrong, and I don't mind admitting it."

The boys slept on in their room, oblivious of everything. George and Dinah sat down at the kitchen table, with the curtains almost drawn so nobody could see them through the big window. Astrid showered and changed into fresh slacks and jersey. When she came out of the bathroom Dinah said belligerently, "You aren't staying alone tonight, you know. You're coming over to the harbor with Ben and me, or you'll go home with Cam or Fletch."

"If it's necessary," said Astrid mildly.

She went out and down toward the shore, knowing that George watched her from behind the curtains. Probably Hobart was right, but she'd never know until she tried it. He had brought back the fishhouse keys and she went in now and stood there with the door pushed wide open, fingering the tools on the bench. Then she sat on the doorstep where the boys had waited that afternoon when she and Kevin went up the steps. There was even a loon out there again, too. She watched it, willing herself not to think of anything else, and after what seemed a long, long time there was a stealthy movement below her among the big, barnacle-encrusted rocks that filled the cribwork of the wharf—something different from crabs, something larger. She didn't get up to investigate, though the skin drew taut on the back of her neck. Then there were slight sounds on the far side of the wharf where there was a seldom-used ladder; footsteps on the planking; and Kevin came around the corner of the fishhouse. His hair was tangled, he was muddy, he was damp, he was scratched and bloody from barnacles. His face was lumpy and blotched, his eyelids swollen from long weeping. She stood up to meet him and he came forward, blind with tears, into her arms.

A fterward
When the police were through with the room and had taken the mattress away, and Cam and Fletch had moved out the other things she wanted never to see again, it was hers to do with as she pleased. It would not be her room again, but the spare room. She fixed up the other room for herself and had the telephone extension moved in there.

Before she shifted her night table, she opened the drawer for the first time that she could remember since Gray had left her, intending to clean out anything left from the past life. The drawer would start out empty.

One of the things was a book of Emily Dickinson's poems that Gray had given her one Christmas. She couldn't bear to destroy it, so it would be tucked away out of sight on a downstairs bookshelf, and maybe in years to come she would open it again. Why then did she torment herself now by looking at Gray's handwriting and the loving inscription on the fly leaf? She never knew the answer, only that she couldn't lay the book aside without opening it.

Under the inscription there was more, written in a rushed, nearly illegible scrawl, but *his*.

"My dearest Astrid—unless you really hate me, please don't divorce me until *we can talk*. This time away should straighten things out if ever they can be straightened out for a fool like me. Give my love to the boys. I love you. As always, Gray."

She saw him, saw the set of his shoulders and the cant of his dark head as he sat on the side of the bed, writing in the book laid open on the nightstand. He kept calling to Dorri not to come upstairs, and this was why. When she started up anyway, he'd slid the book back into the drawer. Then he'd tried to get her out of the room.

If the police searchers had opened the drawer, and they must have, they'd have seen no gun and would have ignored the book. And all this time the note had been there waiting for her.

And now it was clear why Dorri hadn't wanted them to meet. She thought she was losing her hold on him and didn't know how many times more she could use her suicide threat. She may have already been teasing him for a trip somewhere, and he'd finally given in with some reckless idea of giving her the expedition as a farewell gift, which it had turned out to be.

Astrid was beyond weeping as she stared at his writing. She tried to tell herself that he couldn't have been freed of his obsession until Dorri was ready to shake him off; that even if he'd come back home he and Astrid had been driven too far apart. But all she could think of was that he had left this message for her, and Kevin had killed him when the plea was fresh in his mind, when he was thinking of her, when he had just written *I love you.*

I could kill you, Kevin! she thought, knowing that in a sense Kevin had already been killed. *He'll get over it,* Gray had said. Would he remember that, seeing his gun in Kevin's hand?

When she could bear to, when they were all stronger, she would show the note to Fletch and Cam. They had a right to know what had been in his mind. Cam would curse bitterly, but it might ease Fletch a little. Or the irony would make him feel worse.

She put the book away on the top shelf of her closet.

Midsummer
"Are you still going to run away and stop thinking?" Lieutenant Hobart asked her. It was the day after her mother's visit had ended.

"What, take the boys away from their home and their uncles? No," she said. "I'll have the shop taken down, though. We'll have a new workshop in a corner of the barn. Maybe they'll never have to know how their father died, but I'll worry about that when the time comes."

They were at the cove, watching the boys sail new boats in the tide pool. He had brought the boats. The new *Ibex* swung on the haul-off beside the dory.

"It's simple for me," she said. "Well, not exactly that, but more so than it is for Carrie and Rupe and for the Whitehouses." She looked candidly at him, blue eyes to blue, and said, "Sometimes I cry for Kevin as much as for Gray."

Kevin was in the Mental Health Institute at Augusta. She knew that Celia blamed her, even though the Gray–Dorri–Kevin involvement had begun long before Astrid knew of it. But Celia had to blame somebody, since the others were dead.

"Try not to let it get too much for you," said Hobart.

"Don't brood over it. What are you going to do? Do you need to work?"

"Oh yes, we aren't well off, you know." She made a dismissing gesture with her hand. "But I've sold the Audi and that's put away for the boys, we have a little money in the bank, and the house is free and clear, though the taxes are getting to be just slightly less than the national defense budget. The children have Social Security benefits and my mother's putting something by for them. And I'm going to be a handyman."

"A *what?*" His black eyebrows went up the way they did when he was startled.

"A handyman! I'll put in gardens, mow lawns, paint, paper, refinish furniture, wash cars. Maybe house-clean, including windows. Teach your kids to swim—"

"Not mine. I'm not married."

"Oh," she said.

"I was wondering if you'd let me see these boys from time to time." He actually sounded diffident. "I know they've got two wonderful uncles, but there might be a way I could help too, occasionally. I wouldn't be a nuisance, I promise you."

She fastened her hands around her knee and studied him, thinking, He's really very nice, and kind, and, yes, he's ill at ease right now. I'd never have believed it possible.

"I'm not making a pass," he said with dignity.

She grinned. "I know you aren't. You wouldn't. And the boys would feel awful if they didn't see you again."

# ABOUT THE AUTHOR

Brought up in the suburbs of Boston, Elisabeth Ogilvie was exposed to Maine at an early age and caught a bad case of it. She seldom strays far from her habitat, and for good reason: it's as close to heaven as you can get. There's beach-combing; collecting Indian artifacts on her home island, which was an Indian campground for hundreds of years; unusual birds to keep an eye on; the neighboring wood-chuck and the cock pheasant who crows under her windows in the morning like a rooster. Sometimes a moose takes a short-cut through her backyard, and there's mackerel fishing when the spirit moves.

Miss Ogilvie says she wants to spend a year in Scotland when she no longer has an Australian terrier to worry about. In the meantime, what with reading and writing and the whole outdoors, she doesn't have much time to think about travel.